The Awakening- Susan's Path to Sensual Empowerment

Wanda Peters

Published by Wanda Peters, 2024.

THE AWAKENING- SUSAN'S PATH TO SENSUAL EMPOWERMENT

First edition. May 17, 2024.

Copyright © 2024 Wanda Peters.

ISBN: 979-8224362165

Written by Wanda Peters.

Also by Wanda Peters

10 Reasons You Should Cuckold Your Husband
Cruel Wife, Slave Husband
Embracing My Inner Bitch
Erotic Short Stories of Dominance and Submission
My Evil Step-Sister Returns Illustrated
Cuckolded By A Stranger, An Erotic Novel
Cuckolded By His Boss
The Hot Wife Club
Cuckolded and Bound for Punishment
Cuckolded By My Best Friend
Cuckold's Anonymous
An Anniversary To Remember
My Wife's Surprise
Terrified of Bondage A Wife in Peril
Training Her Cuckold Husband
A Little Devil in Georgia
His Mother's Advice
Addicted To High Heels or A Slave To My Wife's Boots
The Huntress
A Wedding to Remember
Evil Under a Western Sky
The Number Four Reason You Should Cuckold Your Husband
Cuckolding The Bootlicker
Bondage and Discipline 101
Tales of Love Romance and Marriage

Tales of Love, Romance and Marriage
The Evil Therapist Returns
Cracks in the Vow Six Stories of Love's Demise
Two Books Of Domination And Legal Thrillers
An Old Flame For Ava
An Interview With An Erotic Writer
Bound For Desire
The Awakening- Susan's Path to Sensual Empowerment

Author's Note:

This book is in its entirety a work of fiction. Any resemblance to anyone living or dead is a coincidence. All images in this book have been AI-generated and have no copywrites attached. As this book is erotic, no one under the age of 18 should read it.

The Awakening- Susan's Path to Sensual Empowerment

Chapter One-Opening Up Susan's Therapy Session

"To be frank, I'm not even certain why I came today, Doctor." Susan began hesitantly.

Dr. Marks regarded her with an understanding smile. "Susan, you knew my fee was $300 per hour when you scheduled this appointment. I'm confident there's some reason you felt compelled to spend that kind of money. We can sit silently for the remainder of our 55 minutes, or you can unburden yourself of what you came here to discuss."

"Alright, though this will sound rather foolish even to me. In most respects, John is the ideal husband. He performs more than his share of household chores and is eager to fulfill my every wish in the bedroom."

"Please, go on," the psychiatrist gently urged.

Susan faltered, grasping for the right words. Though she had just described John as nearly the perfect husband, here she was struggling to articulate that she was utterly bored after only three years of marriage.

"Speak your mind. I can see the gears churning behind those lovely eyes."

So she blurted out precisely what she was thinking. "I'm bored with my marriage."

"Bored in what way?" Dr. Marks inquired.

It was challenging to find the terms to elucidate her dilemma. Seconds crawled by at a torturous pace as she groped for the perfect phrasing. She could feel a flush of embarrassment coloring her complexion and knew she likely resembled a contrite child. The silence was deafening, becoming more than she could withstand.

"Sex," Susan finally uttered the solitary word emerging with effort.

Dr. Marks' face lit up with an enormous grin as she peered intently into Susan's eyes. "Didn't you just tell me he was eager to satisfy your every desire in that arena?"

"That's the crux of it. I don't want to have to instruct him what to do. I'd like him to take charge occasionally."

"Have you communicated this yearning to him?"

"That rather defeats the purpose, doesn't it? I'm certain he could play the part, but that's not what I crave."

"What makes you so convinced he would have to pretend? Perhaps he would relish taking charge but fears offending you if he did."

"I believe that response answers your question. He shouldn't be so timid."

"It seems you have a real predicament," the doctor began. "On one hand, you want your husband to take control in the bedroom, yet you're unwilling to tell him that's your desire. On the other, you're becoming sexually unfulfilled. Have you considered having an affair?"

Susan's mouth gaped in astonishment. "Of course, I haven't contemplated an affair! I'm shocked you would even propose such a thing."

"Then I'll ask again, why did you come to see me today?"

"I don't know, I suppose I hoped you could show me how foolish I've been and tell me to go back and ravish my husband senseless."

"And how would that change your circumstances?" the doctor queried.

"I guess it wouldn't. So I'm back where I started. I presume I'll have to figure this out alone."

"I didn't say I wouldn't assist you. My advice is for you to visit a club I'm familiar with called 'The Power Exchange'. You needn't interact with anyone unless you wish, but you'll have the chance to closely observe those who have willingly relinquished their free will to their sexual partner. If you like what you see, perhaps you could explore further. If not, you will have lost only an evening of your time. Here is the address and their days and hours of operation."

Susan reached out and accepted the information from the doctor. "Thank you, Dr. Marks. I'll consider your suggestion." She moved to the door to leave but before she could open it, Dr. Marks stopped her.

"Oh, and Susan, here is something I think you should wear when you visit the club." She crossed the room and handed Susan a plain paper bag. "Don't open it until you get home."

Chapter Two –Exploration in the Night-Susan's Club Experience

Susan's mind churned as she piloted her sedan through the sleepy suburbs toward home. Dr. Mark's scandalous suggestion of an affair still echoed in her thoughts. Though initially shocked, intrigue now gripped her, refusing to let go. The idea of visiting a club devoted to dominance and submission excited her in a way she never imagined.

Tonight, with Harold at his weekly poker game, the house would be empty. If she was going to explore this club, no better opportunity would arise. Pulling into the driveway, she resolved not to spend the night home alone waiting for Harold's return.

Inside, she rushed to the bag Dr. Mark had given her, gasping when her fingers clasped a thick, studded dog collar. "What is this for?" she wondered, perplexed yet enthralled. Shaking her head, she hurried upstairs to prepare.

After a brisk shower, Susan foraged her closet, debating what to wear. A diaphanous blouse and tiny skirt could flaunt her assets but might attract too much attention. She had no idea what to expect in this foreign place.

After trying several outfits, she selected a conservative pantsuit and low heels. Underneath, though, she donned a black garter belt and bra, keepsakes Harold had never seen. Sheer black stockings followed, eliciting a coy smile as she lightly applied makeup.

Satisfied with looking chic but not overtly sexy, she turned to leave. But the dog collar Dr. Mark gave her called to her from the bed. An irresistible urge compelled her to lift it to her neck. Though it seemed at odds with her modest outfit, she couldn't stop herself from buckling it on. Gazing in the mirror, warmth flushed through her as her cheeks reddened. Shockingly, moisture pooled between her thighs as she mentally referred to her womanhood as her cunt. More wetness followed that profane thought.

She desperately wanted to lock the collar in place. Fighting the urge to fetch a padlock from the garage consumed her. It took supreme effort not to stop at the hardware store for one on her way. These primal desires disturbed and thrilled her.

Somehow she drove to the club's address while battling her collar fixation. The well-lit parking lot overflowed with cars far nicer than hers. She had to park a long walk from the entrance.

Only a handful waited to enter when she arrived. One by one, they were admitted by a brawny doorman. Only when her turn came did she notice the $50 cover charge sign. Mortified, she realized her purse held no cash, only plastic. She offered the doorman a card but he shook his head gruffly, pointing her to an ATM a block away.

As she turned to leave, something clicked on her collar. A strong hand gripped her head to prevent her from looking back. "This bitch is with me, Al," a deep masculine voice asserted.

"Very good, sir," the doorman replied, opening the door for them.

Propelled inside by a push, the collar's tension vanished once the door closed. A man dressed all in shiny black led her by a leash. His tight shirt molded to bulging muscles she longed to caress.

Eyes dropping lower, she admired his firm buttocks and muscular legs, letting a soft sigh escape her lips. A harsh tug on the leash followed. "Keep your eyes up, bitch!" he commanded.

Though she bristled at being called a bitch, Susan couldn't form a rebuttal. Instead, she obeyed, returning her gaze to his strong back. Dying of curiosity about the club, she nevertheless felt compelled to submit to this stranger.

She was startled when he helped her onto a padded bench and unhooked the leash. Relieved yet disappointed to be free of his control, she studied his face. He was the most gorgeous man she'd ever seen. Silky black curls framed stunning onyx eyes that peered into her soul. His full lips made her wonder how they would feel on hers. A hint of stubble shadowed his jaw, tempting her to stroke it.

Realizing she was gawking, she awaited his reprimand. But no displeasure showed on his face. Emboldened, she let her eyes wander over his massive chest and abnormally large hands. She imagined them squeezing her flesh as he pressed against her. Disappointed at the lack of bulge in his pants, she feared her attraction was one-sided.

After a long silence, his velvet voice asked what brought her here tonight. She murmured about filling a prescription, which he dismissed as too clinical. When he offered a tour, she readily agreed, eager to explore this foreign world.

Chiding her for staring, he suggested she look around instead. She realized they were alone in a lounge except for the bartender. "Where is everyone?" she asked.

"We've not gotten to the main club yet. This is just a reception area. If you'll follow me, I'll give you the nickel tour," he offered.

As she rose to accompany him, Susan was struck by the fact she didn't even know his name yet was obeying his every whim. "What should I call you?" she asked timidly.

He smiled. "Hopefully someday you'll call me Master. For now, Rafael will do." He strode towards a large wooden door without waiting for a reply.

Though he didn't clip on the leash or take her hand, Susan followed him eagerly. Stepping through the door, she gasped at the cavernous space beyond. A well-stocked bar lined one wall, but only a few lone stools occupied the ends.

Another wall displayed cages - some vacant, others confining naked men and women. Susan gawked at their exposed bodies on full display. Glancing around, she saw people lounging in plush chairs while others sat on the hard floor, used as human footstools. Though part of her recoiled, the soft folds between her legs dripped with arousal.

Certain there was more to dominance and submission than this, Susan considered asking Rafael for a deeper glimpse. But instead, he abruptly headed for the distant bar without a word, leaving her bewildered. Was he done with her, having gotten her this far? He would have said something, she reasoned.

As she began to rise, a striking couple in shiny black leather cut off her path. Susan could plainly see who held the reins here. The woman's posture collar connected to a harness that forced her bound arms up at a cruel angle. Her bare breasts bulged out of the leather's grip, the nipples clamped and weighted to stretch them downward. Susan winced, even as the sight stirred her desire.

"Eyes down, bitch!" the man snarled venomously.

Susan whipped her head toward him. "Who are you calling a bitch?" she retorted boldly.

"Slaves cannot speak unless asked," he replied sternly.

"Well, if I meet a slave, I'll let them know. Now move aside," she commanded.

The man's face purpled, forehead veins bulging as his hands clenched into fists. Susan's courage faltered as she feared he might strike her.

But then Rafael's dulcet voice interjected, "What's going on here, Murray?"

"Is this your slave, Rafael? You should teach her manners."

"Perhaps I should teach you some? Who made you the club police?" Rafael countered.

The man seethed but his fists unclenched as he turned to leave. Still, he had to have the last word, spitting at Rafael, "A slave should not dress that way. You should be ashamed."

Once alone, Susan thanked Rafael for intervening. "Don't read too much into it," he cautioned. "I'd have done the same for any member. But he wasn't wrong - if you were my slave, I would be ashamed of your attire."

Stung, Susan hung her head briefly before defiance overcame her. "Well, I'm neither your slave nor anyone's. If I embarrass you, perhaps I should leave?"

"You know the way out," he said bluntly, walking away.

Chapter Three – Crossroads of Confession-Susan's Dilemma

With a sinking feeling in her chest, Susan watched Rafael's retreating figure. Her outburst had been rash and now she regretted it deeply. The club that she had been so eager to explore suddenly felt unwelcoming and daunting. She tried to muster the courage to stay and make the most of the night, but the weight of Rafael's words crushed her confidence. With a heavy heart, she turned towards the exit, already feeling like an outsider in this world.

As she stepped outside, the cool night air hit her face like a slap. She took a deep breath, trying to shake off the embarrassment and disappointment that clung to her like a second skin. Leaning against her car, she gazed up at the starry sky, lost in thought.

But just as she was about to retreat into her mind, a voice cut through her reverie. "Are you alright?"

Susan looked up to see a man standing a few feet away, his expression gentle and concerned. She hesitated for a moment, unsure if she should let him in or push him away like she did with everyone else. But something about his sincere concern made her want to open up. So with a sigh, she decided to share the rollercoaster of emotions that had consumed her throughout the evening.

Without realizing it, Susan found herself speaking, her words cascading forth like a waterfall as she poured out the events of the evening to the attentive stranger. He listened with rapt focus, his warm brown eyes encouraging her to unburden her soul.

As Susan spoke, it felt as though a massive weight was lifting from her weary shoulders. Her voice flowed effortlessly like a river rushing over smooth stones.

"I would be honored to escort you back inside if you wish," the man offered his mellow tone soothing Susan's frazzled nerves.

"Thank you, but I think I should return to my home and husband," Susan replied regretfully, a sharp pang of guilt piercing her conscience.

The man reached into his crisp white shirt pocket and produced a sleek onyx business card. "If you change your mind, please don't hesitate to give me a call. My cell number is on the card," he said gently.

Grateful for his kindness, Susan thanked the man, his compassion a bright spot in her turbulent evening. She turned and walked to her car, the click of her heels echoing in the night.

When Susan arrived home, she prayed that Harold would already be asleep. But as her luck would have it, he was wide awake, ensconced in his overstuffed armchair as the TV flickered, casting an eerie glow about the room. As Susan entered, Harold's penetrating gaze raked over her, searching for any hint of impropriety. Susan silently thanked herself for not dressing more provocatively for the club.

She glided across the room to the mahogany cabinet that served as their liquor stash. Taking a petite crystal goblet, she poured herself a splash of velvety red wine and drifted back to the sofa.

Susan took a luxurious sip, the wine bursting with ripe, jammy flavors on her tongue. The silence between her and Harold was oppressive, saturated with unspoken accusations and simmering tension. She knew he was waiting for an explanation, some shred of justification for her late return.

Finally, after an agonizing eternity, Harold cleared his throat abrasively. "Where have you been, Susan? You look like you've been to hell and back."

Susan met his scrutinizing gaze unflinchingly, seeing the caution and curiosity swirling in his slate-grey eyes. She deliberated how much to disclose about the salacious events of the evening, about her foray into the shadowy world of dominance and submission.

"I went to a club," Susan began slowly, carefully selecting her words. "It wasn't what I expected..."

Susan met his gaze, seeing the concern mixed with curiosity in his eyes. She debated how much to reveal about the events of the evening, about her venture into the world of dominance and submission that had taken an unexpected turn.

"I went to a club," Susan began slowly, choosing her words with care. "It wasn't what I expected."

Harold's eyebrows shot up in surprise, but he remained silent, waiting for her to continue.

As Susan recounted the evening's events, she saw a myriad of emotions flicker across Harold's face – disbelief, concern, and a hint of intrigue. He listened intently as she described her interactions with Rafael and the unexpected turn of events that led to her early departure from the club.

When she finished speaking, there was a moment of silence as Harold processed everything she had shared. Finally, he spoke, his voice soft yet full of understanding.

"Thank you for telling me, Susan. I can only imagine how challenging tonight must have been for you," Harold said, reaching out to gently squeeze her hand.

Susan felt a wave of relief wash over her at his words, grateful for his support and compassion. She knew that she could always count on Harold to be there for her, no matter what challenges they faced together.

As they sat in the quiet of their living room, Susan realized that despite the chaos of the evening, she was thankful for the unexpected turn of events. It had brought her closer to Harold in a way she hadn't expected, strengthening their bond and deepening their connection.

"I could try to be the dominant man that you want," Harold offered.

Susan observed Harold's earnest expression, his offer hanging in the air between them. She knew that his willingness to adapt, to step into a role that didn't come naturally to him, stemmed from a place of love and a desire to meet her needs. But she also recognized the truth in her own heart - that dominance couldn't be forced or feigned; it had to be innate, a part of one's being.

Taking a deep breath, Susan reached out and gently clasped Harold's hand. "Thank you for offering, but I need you to understand that dominance isn't something you can simply put on or take off," she began softly.

Harold's gaze searched hers, a mix of emotions swirling in his eyes. "I just want to make you happy, Susan. I'll do whatever it takes."

A surge of affection for her well-meaning husband flooded Susan's heart. She squeezed his hand reassuringly. "I know you would, Harold. But true dominance isn't something that you can become. It is something that you are. Do you understand what I am saying to you?"

"I think so, but what I don't understand is why you want someone to dominate you. And I don't understand what that means. Do you want to be hurt? Are you a masochist?"

Susan could sense Harold's confusion and concern, and she knew she needed to choose her words carefully to help him understand. Taking a deep breath, she replied, "No, Harold, it's not about being hurt or enjoying pain. It's about trust, surrender, and exploring different aspects of intimacy and connection."

Harold furrowed his brows in thought, processing her words slowly. After a moment, he spoke again, his voice tinged with a mix of uncertainty and determination. "I want to understand, Susan. I want to be the partner you need me to be. Show me how to support you in this journey."

Moved by Harold's sincerity and willingness to learn, Susan felt a swell of love for him in her heart. She reached out and took both of his hands in hers, looking into his eyes with gratitude. "Thank you, Harold. Just being open to understanding means more to me than you can imagine."

Chapter Four-Navigating New Horizons-Susan and Harold Seek Counsel

For a time Susan was able to put the idea of being a submissive wife on the back burner. Settling into her work and home life, Susan tried to ignore the nagging voice in the back of her mind that longed for something more. But as the days turned into weeks, that voice grew louder and more insistent, echoing in her thoughts even as she went about her daily routine.

Finally, she decided that she needed to talk with Dr. Marks again. She picked up her phone and made the call. Dr. Mark's nurse answered and after a brief question and answer period set a time for the appointment, with the suggestion that she might want to bring her husband with her.

That night after the dinner dishes had been cleaned and taken care of Susan approached her husband asking if he would be willing to go with her to talk with a marriage counselor.

Harold's initial reaction was one of surprise, his brows furrowing in confusion. "Frankly I was hoping that you had forgotten about the idea of dominance and submission." But after a moment of thought, he nodded slowly. "If it's important to you, Susan, then I'll go with you," he said, his voice tinged with sincerity.

Susan felt a swell of gratitude towards her husband for his willingness to support her. She knew that delving into their relationship dynamics with a marriage counselor would not be easy, but she also knew that it was necessary.

The day of the appointment arrived, and Susan found herself sitting next to Harold in the waiting room of Dr. Marks' office. The air was tense with unspoken words as they both pondered the road ahead.

When they were called into the counselor's office, Dr. Marks greeted them warmly and ushered them to sit on the plush couch facing him.

Susan introduced Harold to Dr. Marks, her voice steady but her heart racing with anticipation. Dr. Marks offered a warm smile and shook Harold's hand before settling back into her chair, her gaze thoughtful as she regarded the couple before him.

"Thank you for coming in today," Dr. Marks began, her tone inviting and calm. "Susan has shared with me that you both have some concerns you'd like to discuss. Why don't we start by each of you telling me a little bit about what's been on your minds lately?"

Susan gently placed her hand on Harold's arm, silently urging him to speak first. After a moment of hesitation, he cleared his throat and began to share his perspective on their relationship. His words were tentative yet sincere as if he were opening up a vulnerable part of himself. He spoke of his deep love for Susan, his confusion over her recent desires for dominance, and his earnest attempts to understand and support her.

As Harold finished speaking, Susan turned to face him, taking his hand in hers and giving it a reassuring squeeze. Then she turned to Dr. Marks, the mediator they had sought out to help them navigate their complicated marriage. "As you know," Susan started, her voice low but steady, "I have been struggling with feelings of inadequacy in our marriage. Not long ago, I confided in you about my desire to explore my submissive side, and at your suggestion, I went to a BDSM club here in town." She took a deep breath before continuing, recounting the events that had transpired with Rafael and another man, and how she ultimately rejected Rafael's idea of human slavery.

Susan hesitated before going any further and Dr. Marks turned to Harold with a curious expression. "Harold," she asked calmly, "Did you know that Susan was planning on going to a BDSM club?"

He shook his head slowly. "Not ahead of time," he admitted, "but she did tell me about it after she got home. Frankly Dr., I don't understand why Susan has these desires. Women have fought for centuries for equal rights with men, and now my wife wants to turn back the clock 50 years. Maybe you can shed some light on why she feels this way."

Dr. Marks remained neutral and professional in her response. "It is not my place to speak for your wife," she said firmly, "I am simply here as a neutral party to help facilitate communication and understanding between the two of you." She turned to Susan, her gaze soft yet probing. "Susan, would you like to share more about your feelings and desires with Harold?"

Susan took a deep breath, steeling herself for the vulnerability of her next words. She turned to Harold, her eyes locking with his in a silent plea for understanding. "Harold, I want you to know that my desire for submission does not stem from a lack of respect for myself or women. I still believe that women should be equal to men in the workplace or politics, but I also believe that trying to wear pants in the marriage relationship is a mistake."

"I don't understand, where are these thoughts coming from?"

"I never did tell you about how I was raised," Susan began.

"My mother wasn't equal with my father in our house and she didn't want to be. I remember my father coming home from a long day's work. He would come into the house, sit in his chair and my mother would immediately go to him, get down on her knees, and help him remove his shoes. She would help him one with his slippers, go get his pipe, light it for him, and then finish making supper for the family. I thought that was strange until I asked her one day why she did it. Her answer was, "Because it makes me happy." Susan let those words hang in the air. "She explained to me that my father worked hard all day to make a living for us and the least that she could do was to make his life easier once he came home."

"I think that I can understand the dynamic relationship that your parents shared. It isn't all that much different from my parents, but I think there is more to your submissive desires than just making a happy home."

"There is more to the story of my mother and father. My mother wasn't just submissive to my father in the ways that I have related to you. She also was submissive in the bedroom."

"You mean that she allowed your father to take the lead in lovemaking, is that it Susan?"

"It went well beyond that," Susan began. "I asked Mom about how deep her submission to my father went and after much probing, she opened up and told me. She said that when they were first married, she was more concerned with her orgasms, than how she got them.

Mom had learned that the best orgasms she ever had were when she allowed my father to do as he pleased with her. Sometimes he would be gentle and loving, other times he was rough and demanding. She soon learned that it didn't matter how she got them, only that I did get them As Susan shared these intimate details with Harold and Dr. Marks, she could see the mix of shock, confusion, and intrigue on their faces. She continued her voice steady but laced with vulnerability.

"I know it may be hard to understand, Harold," Susan murmured, reaching for his hand as she spoke, "but my mother's submission to my father wasn't about giving up her power or independence. It was a choice she made out of love and a desire to please him, just as he worked hard to provide for our family."

Harold's expression softened as he listened to Susan's words. There was a flicker of realization although he was still unsure as to how far Susan wanted to take this idea.

Dr. Marks looked at the couple and announced that she would like to speak with Harold alone.

Chapter Five-Harold's Story

Susan got up and headed for the door, looking back at her husband, wondering what he might reveal. When the door had closed behind her, Dr. Marks addressed her husband. "Harold I have been watching you. Most men would be over the moon to find out that their wife wanted to wait on them hand and foot but you seem disappointed. Can you explain that?"

Harold looked down deep in contemplative thought. "I suppose that my disappointment lies in the fact that I cannot be the type of husband that Susan wants."

"Why do you feel that way," the psychologist asked.

"I have always believed in the movement of women seeking equal rights with men. I can't just sit in my easy chair while my wife waits on me hand and foot. The guilt would eat me alive."

Dr. Marks nodded, understanding Harold's internal struggle. "It's commendable that you hold such strong beliefs about equality, Harold. But it's also important to recognize that marriage is a partnership, and different couples have unique dynamics that work for them. Susan's desires may not align with societal norms, but they are valid in the context of your relationship."

Harold sighed, running a hand through his hair in frustration. "I just can't wrap my head around it. How can I reconcile my principles with what Susan is asking for?"

Dr. Marks couldn't help but feel that Harold was holding something back, something more than his belief in equality. "I can't help but think that you aren't telling me the entire story, Harold. I can't help either of you if I don't understand the complete dynamic of your relationship."

Harold looked at her sheepishly. "It is just that I can't be dominant."

"Why is that Harold?" she asked him although she knew the answer.

"Because I want to be submissive to my wife," he replied.

Dr. Marks raised an eyebrow, intrigued by Harold's confession. She had suspected there was more to their dynamic than met the eye, but this revelation added a new layer of complexity to their marriage.

"Harold, it's perfectly normal to have desires that deviate from societal expectations," she began gently. "Exploring your submissive side doesn't diminish your beliefs in equality; it simply means you have a different way of expressing your love and intimacy."

Harold shifted in his seat, seemingly relieved to finally voice his inner struggle. "I've always felt guilty for wanting Susan to take control of our relationship. It goes against everything I've been taught about being a man. But seeing her embrace her submissive desires has made me realize that I have my own needs too."

Dr. Marks nodded thoughtfully, noting the weight that had been lifted off Harold's shoulders with his admission. "It's essential for both partners to feel fulfilled and understood in a relationship. Unfortunately in your marriage, you can't both be submissive. In every relationship one is dominant and the other submissive."

"Then what is the answer, do we need to consider divorce?"

"That would be a very drastic solution to the problem. I think that you need to explore the dynamics of power exchange with your wife, not as a dominant but as a fellow submissive."

"I don't understand how that is possible," Harold replied.

I think that Susan met a man at the BDSM club who might be able to help with that.

Chapter Six – Unveiling Desires

Susan had indeed met a man at the BDSM club who went by the name of Master Alexander. He was known for his expertise in guiding couples through the intricacies of power exchange dynamics. After much discussion with Susan, Harold reluctantly agreed to meet with Master Alexander to see if he could help them navigate their desires and conflicting needs.

The meeting took place in Master Alexander's impeccably decorated dungeon, a space that exuded both authority and comfort. Harold felt a mixture of apprehension and curiosity as he sat across from Master Alexander, who regarded him with keen eyes.

"Harold, thank you for joining us today," Master Alexander began in a calm, reassuring tone. "Susan has shared with me some of the challenges you both are facing in your relationship. It's commendable that you are willing to explore this side of yourselves together."

Harold shifted uneasily in his seat, unsure of what to expect. "I've always believed in equality and mutual respect in a relationship. But I also want to understand Susan's need to be submissive."

"Susan, do you remember the night we met outside of the club?"

"I do sir," she replied.

"And do you remember telling me about meeting Rafael and what he said about your style of dress?"

"Yes sir, he said that if I was his slave he would be ashamed of me for the way that I was dressed."

"Please tell us how you were dressed."

"I was wearing a yellow pantsuit with low heels."

"Why did you think that Rafael objected to that?"

"I can only assume that he thought that I was covering up too much of my body," was Susan's reply.

"So knowing that why are you dressed as you are today?" Alexander asked Harold.

"I am sorry Master, I wasn't given any instructions as to how I should dress. I did however decide to wear a short skirt instead of pants."

"I can understand that, now unbutton your blouse."

"Wait just a minute", Harold broke in.

Have you decided that you don't want to learn about your wife's desire to be submissive, Harold?"

"No, but I do object to having you treat my wife like a whore."

"Susan is that how you think that I am treating you?"

"No, Master, I think you are just testing my level of submission." And with that, she began unbuttoning her blouse.

Harold was shocked to see that she was wearing a bright red bra under her blouse.

Susan could feel her heart racing as Harold's accusatory words hung in the air. She regretted wearing the bright red bra that Master Alexander had picked out for their session, knowing how much it would anger her husband. But a part of her also enjoyed provoking his jealousy.

"I did have an idea, but I didn't think you would react like this," she admitted, avoiding his gaze. "I wanted to explore my submission with someone else, but I never wanted to hurt you."

Harold's face contorted in pain and betrayal. "Is that what this is about? Being submissive to another man?"

Susan bit her lip, feeling both guilty and exhilarated by the thought of obeying Master Alexander's every command. "I didn't mean for it to happen like this. I just wanted us to try something new together."

"Well, clearly that didn't work out," Harold snapped back, pulling away from her touch.

Susan felt tears prick in her eyes as she struggled to explain herself. "I never meant to cheat on you. I just...wanted to see if this was something we could do together."

Harold's expression softened slightly, but there was still hurt in his eyes. "How long has this been going on?"

Susan looked down, ashamed to admit the length of time she had been seeing Master Alexander behind Harold's back. When she finally met his gaze again, he seemed almost disgusted with her.

"Do you honestly think I would have an affair with him?" she asked, trying to defend herself.

Harold shook his head, disappointment was evident in his voice. "It doesn't matter anymore. If this is the kind of marriage we have, then maybe we shouldn't be together."

Susan's heart sank at his words, torn between wanting to make things right with Harold and exploring her newfound desires with Master Alexander. "Please don't leave me," she pleaded weakly.

Harold sighed, looking conflicted. "I'll leave, but I want you to come with me. This isn't the kind of life I want for us."

Susan's mind raced as she thought about the ultimatum Harold had just given her. But in the end, she knew what she wanted; even if it meant losing her husband, she couldn't give up this new side of herself that Master Alexander had awakened. "I'm sorry, Harold," she said softly. "I have to stay and see where this goes."

Harold shook his head sadly and then got up and headed for the door.

Chapter Seven – Susan's Surrender

As the door closed behind her husband, Susan turned back toward her Master. "I am so sorry that this happened. I had hoped that Harold would understand my needs and perhaps share them."

"Not too many men could accept watching his wife disrobe in front of another man," Master Alexander told her. "But, now that he is gone we can continue with your lesson. Take off the blouse and skirt so that I can see the rest of your lingerie."

"Yes, Master," Susan replied as she began to pull her blouse from the waistband of her skirt. She took her time unbuttoning the side button of her skirt, hoping to arouse the man that she had chosen over her husband.

Susan was soon down to her bra and panties. Master Alexander's eyes burned with desire as he took in Susan's body, clothed only in the red lingerie he had chosen for her. "You've done well so far," he whispered, a teasing smile on his lips. "But now it's time to truly submit to me."

Susan's heart raced as she realized what he meant, the words hanging in the air between them. She knew what was coming, and part of her yearned for it, while another part trembled in fear. But she could feel her submissive nature taking over, and she knew she couldn't resist Master Alexander's commands.

Slowly, she reached behind her and unhooked her bra, letting it fall to the floor. Her breasts were exposed, bare, and vulnerable, and she felt a rush of exhilaration at the thought of surrendering them to Master Alexander's touch.

Next, he watched as she slipped off her panties, revealing her wet pussy. Master Alexander's eyes darkened with lust, and he approached her, his hands reaching out to touch her naked form.

"You are so beautiful," he murmured, his fingers tracing the contours of her body. "Now, let's see how well you can follow my commands."

Susan's heart pounded in her chest as she met his gaze, her desire and fear mixed in a potent cocktail. She knew what was coming, but she also knew that she had to trust Master Alexander, to give herself to him completely.

Master Alexander moved closer to Susan, his eyes never leaving her exposed body and pooling desire. She was vulnerable, yet willing—a combination that set his blood alight. He traced the outline of her nipples with one large hand, watching as they puckered under his touch. "Your tits are beautiful," he growled, pinching lightly, then harder when she whimpered in pleasure.

He slid his other hand down between her legs, spreading them wider apart. His fingers danced over the moist folds of her pussy, parting them to reveal the pink treasure within. A low growl escaped his lips as he explored the slick wetness there—her essence coating his fingers.

"That's my good girl," he praised huskily when she moaned at his touch. His fingers dove deeper into her cunt, seeking out more of the warmth and wetness held within. He felt her clench around him, her arousal growing with each intimate touch of his fingertips against her heated flesh.

"Please...Master," Susan pleaded breathlessly as Master Alexander continued to play this maddening symphony on her body. Her chest heaved with anticipation while ribbons of pure need curled tightly in the pit of her stomach.

But it wasn't enough for Master Alexander; he wanted more—he needed more. His hand left her breast only to resurface between their bodies. The heady scent of raw sex filled the room as he forced two thick fingers inside Susan's quivering hole.

"Fuck... so tight," Alexander grunted as he began pumping hard and fast into her drenched core. The sounds of their skin slapping together echoed in their shared space adding another layer of eroticism to an already lust-drenched atmosphere.

Susan cried out, a symphony of pleasure-pain in every gasp and plea escaping from between clenched teeth. Each thrust made her feel fuller than before - overwhelmed by sensations she could barely comprehend. She felt Master Alexander's fingers curl just right, hitting that sweet spot deep inside her time and time again.

"Scream for me, Susan," he ordered hotly. His voice was rough with carnal need a sound that had her clenching around his thrusting digits. Each plunge of his hand sent jolts of raw pleasure careening through her body in wave after agonizing wave.

"Fuck... don't stop," she gasped out with a broken sob as the tension continued to build within her. Her body grew taut as a bowstring under his expert manipulation - the overwhelming pressure building until she thought she would burst from its intensity.

"Come for me, Susan," Alexander commanded again; his dark eyes locked onto hers as he doubled the pace of his thrusting fingers. He watched as she came undone beneath him - her face a mask of pleasure as she screamed his name into their shared space.

The sight of her climax sparked something primitive in him—his arousal spiking dangerously high. "Your cunt is mine to take, remember?" he growled huskily as he positioned himself at her entrance, ready to claim her fully and brutally.

Her whispered "Yes..." was all he needed.

"I am going to fuck you now, slut," he told her.

Somehow his calling her a slut seemed right to her. "Yes, Master," she breathed, her voice trembling with anticipation. She could feel her pussy dripping wet at his words, her body yearning for him to claim her.

Master Alexander positioned himself between her legs, his erection straining against his pants as he gazed down at her vulnerable form. His eyes locked with hers, and she saw a hunger in his gaze that matched her own.

He reached down and tugged at the waistband of his pants, pulling them down and revealing his hard cock. Susan's heart raced as she watched him step out of his pants and boxers, leaving him fully naked and ready for her.

Without a word, he positioned himself at her entrance, his cockhead pressing against her tight, wet slit. Susan let out a low moan, her body trembling with anticipation. She reached back and grabbed onto the bench for support, her pussy clenching around his cock as he began to slowly push inside her.

"That's it, Susan," he growled, his voice deep and rough. "Take my cock. You're mine now, and I'm going to show you just how much I want you."

Slowly, he started to thrust, his cock sliding deeper and deeper into her wet, tight pussy. Susan gasped, her breath catching in her throat as she felt his erection stretching her open, filling her up in a way she had never felt before.

"Oh, Master," she moaned, her voice breaking. She felt herself creaming around his cock, her body convulsing as she came harder than she ever had before.

Master Alexander groaned, his cock pulsing inside her as he filled her with his seed. He held onto her hips, his body shaking as he rode out his orgasm.

Finally, he collapsed onto her, his body still trembling with pleasure. Susan lay beneath him, her heart pounding in her chest as she basked in the afterglow of their intense lovemaking.

"Thank you, Master," she whispered, her voice full of gratitude and desire. "I didn't know I could feel this way before."

He smiled down at her, his eyes shining with a possessiveness that she found both intimidating and thrilling. "You won't forget this, Susan. I have plans for you."

She nodded, her eyes wide with a mix of fear and excitement. Anticipation. That was the word that best described how Susan felt as she sat on the edge of the bench, her heart pounding in her chest and her pussy damp with anticipation. She had never felt this way before, never been so overcome with desire for someone else. But there was something about Master Alexander that made her want to surrender completely to him, to give herself to him in a way she had never given to anyone before.

As he stood before her, his eyes dark with lust and possession, she could feel herself trembling with a mixture of fear and excitement. He was so different from anyone she had ever been with, so Dominant and commanding. She had always been drawn to that kind of power, the idea of submitting to someone who could take control and make her feel alive in ways she never thought possible.

"Okay, Susan," he said, his voice deep and authoritative. "From now on, you will call me Master.

Susan's heart raced at his words, the weight of his dominance sinking deep into her being. She hesitated for a moment before nodding, feeling a thrill run through her at the thought of surrendering herself to him completely.

"Master," she whispered, testing the word on her lips, feeling a rush of exhilaration at the taboo of it all. His eyes sparked with satisfaction at her compliance, and he took a step closer, his presence overwhelming her senses.

He reached out a hand to cup her chin, tilting her face up to meet his gaze. "Good girl," he praised in a low, husky tone that sent shivers down her spine.

As he leaned in to claim her lips in a possessive kiss, Susan felt a wave of desire wash over her, mingled with a sense of liberation she had never experienced before. In that moment, she knew she had found something she had been searching for—a connection that transcended the boundaries of ordinary intimacy.

Their embrace spoke volumes, each touch and caress carrying the weight of their unspoken desires. And as they lingered in each other's arms, enveloped in a world where passion and power intertwined, Susan realized that this was just the beginning of a journey into the depths of submission and ecstasy, unlike anything she had ever known.

Chapter Eight-The Confession

Susan emerged from the dark, damp dungeon, her mind a whirlwind of conflicting emotions. The cool air outside only served to amplify the intensity of her thoughts. Master Alexander, dressed impeccably as always, guided her into his sleek car. As she sank into the plush leather seat, he made sure she was buckled in before closing her door with a sense of finality.

Silent and tense, they drove away from their secret meeting spot. Susan couldn't help but notice how effortlessly Master Alexander exuded an air of control and power, both in and out of the bedroom. But now, as they sat in the quiet car, his hand occasionally brushing against her thigh, she couldn't shake off the feeling of unease that gnawed at her insides.

"You did exceptionally well tonight," he said smoothly, breaking the silence. "I can tell you thoroughly enjoyed yourself."

Susan couldn't help but blush at his praise, but it also sparked a flicker of guilt within her. She had never been one to submit so willingly to someone else's desires, but with Master Alexander, it came naturally.

"Thank you," she murmured in response.

"But now," he continued, his voice taking on a serious tone, "it's time for me to ask something important of you."

Susan's heart skipped a beat as she braced herself for whatever request he might make. For all his charm and seduction, she knew that Master Alexander expected complete honesty and transparency from her.

"What is it?" she asked hesitantly.

"I need to know everything," he said firmly. "About your past, your desires, your fears. Nothing can be hidden between us if we are to move forward in our relationship."

Susan felt a surge of panic rising within her. She had never been asked to reveal such intimate details about herself before. Would he still accept her once he knew everything?

"Master..." she started, unsure of how to respond.

"I need to know, Susan," he pressed, his gaze intense and unwavering. "It's not a request, it's a requirement."

Feeling like she had no choice, Susan took a deep breath and began to share her deepest secrets with Master Alexander. She spoke of her troubled upbringing and the scars it left on her sense of self-worth.

Before she knew it, they had arrived at her house. Turning to face him, she couldn't help but feel both grateful and conflicted.

"Thank you for today," she said sincerely. "I have never felt more free in my life."

He raised an eyebrow in question. "And what will you tell Harold?"

Susan hesitated, torn between loyalty to Master Alexander and honesty with her husband. The internal struggle was evident on her face as she finally answered,

"It will depend on how much he wants to know. But I won't lie to him."

Master Alexander raised a knowingly arched eyebrow at her response. He understood the complexities of her situation, but he also knew that making her choose between him and Harold would only lead to complications. Instead, he decided to change the subject.

"What do you plan to do now?" he asked a curious note in his voice.

Susan bit her lip, considering her answer. Her heart was still pounding from their intense session, and she felt both exhilarated and overwhelmed.

"I don't know yet," she admitted honestly. "I need some time to process everything that has happened tonight, to think about what it means for me and my relationship with Harold."

A small smile tugged at the corners of Master Alexander's mouth. He could see she was struggling, trying to reconcile her newfound desires with her existing life. But he also knew that if she truly wanted to explore this kinky lifestyle, then he would be there for her.

As they reached the door Susan turned and again thanked the man that had given her so much pleasure. "Will I see you again?" she asked hopefully.

Without replying he pulled her into his arms and lowered his lips to hers.

It wasn't a deep passionate kiss just a reminder of what they had shared that day. "Yes, we will be seeing each other again and soon." With that, he turned and walked back to his car without looking back.

Chapter Nine-Confronting Harold

As Susan enters her house, the weight of the night's events hangs heavy on her mind. With each step, she rehearses the words she will use to explain her encounter with Master Alexander to Harold. The air is thick with tension, anticipation, and a tinge of anxiety as she prepares to reveal a side of herself she had kept hidden for so long. How will Harold react to her newfound desires and vulnerability? Only time will tell as Susan takes a deep breath and crosses the threshold, ready to lay bare her truth and confront the consequences of her choices.

The air inside the house was thick with tension, a stark contrast to the peaceful facade it presented. Susan's emotions were swirling like a hurricane, threatening to consume everything in their path. Harold sat in the living room, lost in his book, oblivious to the impending storm about to hit him.

"Harold," Susan's voice trembled as she spoke, "can we talk?"

He looked up from his book, concern etched on his face as he saw the turmoil in her eyes. "What's wrong?" he asked.

Susan took a deep breath, trying to calm the frantic beating of her heart. "I need to tell you something," she said, her voice wavering, "something that might change everything between us."

Confusion furrowed Harold's brow. "What do you mean?"

Summoning all her courage, Susan forced herself to speak the words she had been dreading. She shared the entire story with Harold - about her encounter with Master Alexander, her newfound desires, her fears, and her struggles with her past. She bared it all to him, including the fact that she had given herself over to another man and surrendered her body to him.

Harold sat there, stunned. The world around him seemed to shrink, and all he could hear was the pounding in his ears. How could Susan confess such things to him? It felt like a punch to the gut. "I don't know what to say," he managed to mutter, his voice barely audible. "This isn't us."

Susan shook her head, tears streaming down her face. "I know, Harold. I never meant for things to get this far. But Master Alexander... he... he made me feel things I've never felt before. And I just... I couldn't resist him."

Harold felt his heartbreak. He loved Susan more than anything in the world, but this... this was too much. He struggled to find the words. "I don't understand, Susan. How could you do this to us?"

Susan's voice faltered. "I don't know, Harold. I'm so sorry. I never meant to hurt you."

He got up from the chair, pacing back and forth. "Why did you bring me into this?"

Susan wrapped her arms around herself, her body shaking. "Because you're my husband, Harold. I can't keep anything from you. I had to tell you."

"But why him?" Harold demanded, anger creeping into his voice. "Why Master Alexander?"

Susan lowered her head, unable to look him in the eye. "It was a mistake. for me to believe that I could only go so far. I thought it would be something fun and exciting, but it's grown into something more. I felt free, Harold. He made me feel alive."

Harold's heart raced as he tried to process Susan's words. Hurt and confusion swirled inside him as he struggled to understand how his loving, gentle wife could suddenly crave a dominant man. Part of him wanted to hold onto their marriage, to try and understand and fulfill her desires. But the other part felt betrayed and angry that she had kept this hidden from him for so long. The thought of being her cuckold made his stomach turn, but the thought of losing her was even worse. His mind was torn and he didn't know what to do or say next.

"Is it over, Susan?

Susan hesitated, trying to find the right words to say. This was the moment she had been dreading, the moment where she would have to face the consequences of her choices.

"I don't know what I expected, Harold," she said honestly. "I don't know what it is about Master Alexander that drew me to him. But I can't deny the emotions he evoked in me. I can't deny the things he taught me about myself."

"So you are telling me that it isn't over, that you are going to continue to see him while I do what?"

"You can still be a part of this, Harold. You say that you have a submissive side of your own. Can't you consider exploring that side of yourself with me and Master Alexander?"

Harold looked at her with disbelief. "Explore my submissive side with you and Master Alexander? You can't be serious."

"I am, Harold. I know it's a lot to take in. But I'm asking you to see the possibility of this. It could bring us closer together if we navigate it the right way."

Harold took a deep breath, trying to process everything Susan had said. He knew he loved her, but the idea of sharing her with another man, especially one who had already taken her, was too much to bear.

"I'm not sure if I can do that, Susan," he said quietly, trying to keep the hurt out of his voice. "I need some time to think about this."

Susan nodded, understanding the gravity of the situation. "Of course, Harold. I'm not asking you to make a decision right now. I just wanted to be honest with you. This is who I am, and I can't go back to the way things were before."

The silence between them was deafening, filled with unspoken words and unresolved feelings. Harold looked at Susan, his heart aching for the love they once shared and the prospects of what could be.

"I need to talk with someone about all this, maybe Dr. Marks."

"I think that is a wonderful idea," Susan began. "Maybe she can add some clarity to our situation. Would you like me to go with you?"

"No, I prefer to go alone. Maybe I can talk more freely if it is just her and I."

"I understand, Harold. And I will support you no matter what you decide to do."

Chapter Ten-Harold Seeks Counsel

Dr. Marks rearranged her schedule when she heard how desperate Harold was to speak with her. So two days after Susan's trist with Master Alexander, Harold walked into Dr. Marks' office. The receptionist told him to take a seat and that the Doctor would be with him shortly.

Harold took a seat, noticing the magazines neatly stacked on the table between the chairs. He selected one about fishing and began to leaf through the pages. He had just begun to read an article about a large bass that was caught in a reservoir in Alabama when the inner office door opened and his name was called.

He set the magazine down and looked up to see a very nice-looking older woman standing in the doorway. He was surprised to see that she was wearing high black boots, today.

Howard set the magazine down rose from his chair and started towards the woman. She smiled and waved him into her office.

"It is good to see you, Harold. How have you been?"

"I have been better, thank you. Actually, that is why I am here today."

The Doctor points Harold to a large armchair and then chooses a smaller office chair to sit in herself.

As she gracefully crosses her legs, Harold's gaze is immediately drawn to her boots. The smooth, dark leather hugs her feet and calves like a second skin. He can't help but feel a slight tingle in his stomach as he imagines the possibilities of what he could do with those boots. His mind wanders to thoughts of running his hands over them, feeling the texture and warmth of the material against his skin. The scent of leather fills his nose, making him almost salivate at the thought.

Harold's gaze lingers on her boots, his eyes tracing the sleek lines and polished leather. They are like a magnet, drawing him in and filling him with desire. He struggles to tear his gaze away, forcing himself to look up at her face.

"No, I'm fine," he stammers, unable to hide the flush creeping up his neck.

She can see right through his lies. She has dealt with men like him before - men with an insatiable fetish for women's boots. In fact, she purposely chose these knee-high boots for today's encounter with Harold. She wants to push him to admit his submissive tendencies, to give in to his desires, and to worship her boots.

Why don't you tell me why you needed to see me this morning."

Harold's grip tightens on the armrests of his chair as he takes a deep breath, steeling himself for the words he knows he needs to say. "Do you remember the last time that Susan and I came to see you?"

The memory of that visit flashes through his mind, igniting a surge of anger and fear in his chest. "Yes, of course," Dr. Marks responds calmly. "Does this visit involve that?"

Harold nods, his jaw clenched tightly. "You told us that perhaps Susan should call the man that she had talked with outside the BDSM club. Well, she did that and set up an appointment for the two of us to go talk with him."

"And how did that work out?" Dr. Marks asks, her eyes narrowing slightly.

"Not too well for me, I'm afraid," Harold admits with a shake of his head. "We had barely entered his dungeon when he demanded that Susan unbutton her blouse. I...I wanted to put a stop to that right then, but Susan wouldn't have it." His voice trembles with suppressed rage and frustration.

Dr. Marks leans forward, her expression intent. "And how did that make you feel?" she presses.

A wave of humiliation and helplessness washes over Harold as he recalls the way Susan had dismissed him so easily in favor of pleasing this stranger in a dark dungeon. His fists clench at his sides as he grits his teeth and forces out the words: "It made me feel like less than nothing."

"Less than nothing," Dr. Marks repeats softly. She regards Harold with a sympathetic look, understanding the depth of his emotions. "It seems like you're struggling with feelings of helplessness and inadequacy."

"Yes," Harold agrees, his voice barely above a whisper. "I feel powerless to protect Susan from this man and his demands, and it's eating away at me."

"Well, Harold," the therapist begins, "it's clear that you're in a difficult situation. But it's also important for you to remember that your feelings are valid, and it's okay to feel this way. The key is to find a way to channel those feelings into something positive."

"But how do I do that?" Harold asks, looking lost. "I feel like I have no control over the situation."

"You may not have control over Susan's choices," Dr. Marks says, "but there are things you can do to empower yourself and take charge of your own life. You can start by exploring your desires and boundaries, perhaps even learning more about BDSM and the role it could play in your life."

Harold's brow furrows as he considers her words. "Perhaps you're right," he says slowly. "I never thought about it like that. Maybe I could find some comfort in exploring my desires and boundaries."

Dr. Marks nods encouragingly. "That's a great first step. If you're interested in exploring BDSM further, there are many resources available. There are books, websites, and even local communities that can help you learn more about the scene."

"That sounds like a lot to take in," Harold admits, looking down at his hands. "But maybe it's time for me to take control of my own life and figure out what I want."

"Can you please explain what occurred after you left Susan alone with Master Alexander?" the doctor inquired, causing a knot to form in Harold's stomach.

"I don't know for sure, but according to Susan, she gave in to his darkest desires and allowed him to use her body like a common prostitute," Harold replied, struggling to keep the bitterness out of his voice.

The doctor raised an eyebrow. "Is that how Susan described it, or is that how you see it?"

Harold hesitated, unsure of how to answer. Was he just projecting his feelings onto Susan's experience? Or was she truly a victim in this situation?

"Her words did not include that particular term. Instead, she described the experience as a liberation like no other. She spoke of Master Alexander as if he had unlocked a hidden realm of ecstasy, igniting desires she never knew existed. As a devout Christian woman, I couldn't help but feel discomfort at her open admission."

Harold, can you tell me what you expected would happen when you left your submissive wife with a dominant man? Did you think that they would just sit and talk?" Dr. Marks asked.

"No," Harold replied, his face flushing deeper with embarrassment. "I mean, I didn't think about it. I was just so concerned about Susan's safety that I...I guess I didn't want to consider what might happen."

"Well, it's natural to be worried about your wife's safety," the doctor said gently. "But you also need to trust her choices and understand that a lot of what she experienced was consensual and part of her exploration. Just like you're exploring your feelings with me now."

Harold sighed, a mixture of relief and resignation washing over him. "I see what you're saying, but it's still difficult to accept."

"I understand, Harold," Dr. Marks assured him. "This is a journey, and it takes time and patience to work through such complex emotions. You're doing well to come here but I don't think that you are being honest with me. Didn't you know that your wife would end up having a sexual encounter with Master Alexander? Be honest, weren't you hoping that was what would happen?"

Her words left him momentarily speechless, but Dr. Marks sensed that she had reached a vulnerable moment in their discussion. "Harold," she said gently, "it's okay if you had certain desires or expectations. What matters now is how you navigate this experience and move forward. Do you want to continue talking about what you hope to achieve from our sessions?"

Harold took a deep breath, his gaze fixed on the floor. "I...I don't know," he admitted. "I suppose I want to find a way to accept Susan's desires and support her, even if they're different from mine."

Dr. Marks nodded in understanding. "That's a great starting point, Harold. And remember, it's not about agreeing with everything your wife does, but respecting her choices and understanding her motivations. This can be challenging, but it's an important part of building a strong and healthy relationship."

"I think we need to delve deeper into what happened with Master Alexander and Susan. You say that you wanted to protect your wife, but you left her alone with another man regardless. So tell me what did you do once you left the dungeon?"

Harold looked down in shame remembering how he had gone home, taken off all his clothes, laid down on top of the comforter on the bed, and slowly masturbated thinking about what Master Alexander was doing to his wife.

But, how could he admit something like that to Dr. Marks?

He nervously fidgeted with his hands, struggling to find the words. "It was...it was a strange feeling, Doctor. One moment I was filled with rage and anxiety, and the next, I was...aroused. I don't know why, but the thought of Susan being with Master Alexander, experiencing things I could only dream of, it excited me." He hesitated, then added, "I know it sounds sick and twisted, but I couldn't help it. It was like a part of me wanted her to stay with him, to experience more. It's not like I wanted her to replace me, but the thought of her being fulfilled sexually and exploring her desires while I stood by helplessly was...it was overwhelming."

Dr. Marks studied Harold carefully, her expression thoughtful. "It's natural for you to feel conflicted, Harold. These feelings may make you uncomfortable, but they're also part of who you are. Looking back on what happened do you wish that you had stayed and watched Susan and Master Alexander making love?"

Harold looked at her incredulously. "Why did you use that phrase, making love?" he asked her. "I don't see how love had anything to do with the raw display of carnal desires and control."

"I understand where you're coming from, Harold," Dr. Marks said gently. "And I'm not trying to dismiss the darker aspects of what happened. Would you have felt better had a used the word fucking instead?"

Harold was shocked but the more he thought about it that was what they were doing. It had nothing to do with Susan's love for Master Alexander or her lack of love for him, it was just a deep carnal desire, hers to be dominated and his to dominate her.

But still, the thought of Susan being with another man, let alone being dominated by him, was eating away at him. He didn't want to admit it, but there was a part of him that wanted to see it for himself, to witness the scene that he had missed out on.

Shamefully, he said, "Yes, maybe. I'm not proud of these thoughts, but it feels like part of the truth. I want to know what happened. I need to see it with my own eyes."

Dr. Marks nodded, understanding the depth of Harold's struggle. "You're in a difficult situation, Harold. But it's also important for you to find a way to process these feelings and come to terms with what happened."

"I don't know how to do that, Doctor. I feel like I'm drowning in confusion and desire," Harold admitted, his voice pleading with her.

"You can start by going home and admit to your wife, what you did that day and how you truly felt about what she was doing."

Do you expect me to tell my wife that I was masturbating to the thought of what she was doing with another man? I can't do that. She would hate me."

"Why did you come here today if you are not willing to take my suggestions?" Dr. Marks asked him.

Harold felt a pang of guilt at the doctor's words. "I don't know," he whispered, his voice barely above a whisper. "I just... felt like I needed to talk to someone about all this."

"And you have," Dr. Marks said, nodding. "But to truly move forward, you need to be willing to face the truth of your feelings and actions. You can't continue to hide behind a facade of protectiveness and concern for Susan when you're just as caught up in your desires."

Harold shook his head, struggling to come up with an answer. "I don't know how to do that," he admitted. "I don't know how to separate my feelings for Susan from what I did that day, or how to tell her what I did without her hating me."

Dr. Marks' voice was laced with frustration as she glared at Harold. "Why did you even bother coming here if you're not willing to listen to my suggestions?" Her tone was sharp, cutting through the air like a knife.

Harold shifted uncomfortably in his seat, feeling the weight of her words heavy on him. He had come seeking help for his submissive tendencies, but now he wasn't sure if he could handle this kind of therapy.

But Dr. Marks wasn't finished yet. "You said you wanted to be submissive to your wife," she continued, her tone softening slightly. "Well, how about being submissive to me?" A mischievous glint flashed in her eyes as she leaned closer to him.

Harold's breath caught in his throat as he looked into her eyes, unsure of what she was implying. Did she mean that she would dominate him? His heart started racing, both afraid and exhilarated by the thought.

"I'm not sure what you mean," he stammered, trying to regain some control over the situation.

A sly smile spread across Dr. Marks' lips as she stood up from her chair and walked towards him. "Do you like my boots, Harold?" Her voice was low and seductive, sending shivers down his spine.

Harold's eyes widened at the sight of the tall black leather boots that reached up to Dr. Marks' thighs. "They're very nice," he replied weakly, feeling small and insignificant under her intense gaze.

Dr. Marks chuckled, shaking her head. "Is that really how you would describe them? I noticed you staring at them earlier. You couldn't take your eyes off of them." She paused, leaning in close enough for Harold to smell the rich leather scent emanating from her boots. "What were you thinking? What do you want to do to these boots right now?" Her voice was like honey, tempting and alluring.

Harold's mind raced with forbidden thoughts as he imagined himself on his knees, worshiping her boots. The mere thought of it made him salivate, his body betraying him.

"Go ahead," Dr. Marks whispered, almost reading his thoughts. "Get down on your knees and crawl to me. Show me your submission."

Harold's breath caught in his throat, his heart pounding in his chest as he hesitated for a moment. But something about the way Dr. Marks looked at him, the way her boots glistened in the light, pulled him in.

Without another thought, Harold sank to his knees, his eyes never leaving the boots. Dr. Marks watched him closely, her expression unreadable.

"Touch them," she whispered, her voice sending shivers down his spine. "Feel the leather, smell it, taste it if you dare."

Harold's hands shook slightly as he reached out, his fingers grazing the smooth surface of the boots. He closed his eyes, inhaling deeply, feeling the rich scent of leather filled his nostrils. It was unlike anything he had ever experienced before.

"Good," Dr. Marks said, her voice a mixture of approval and challenge. "Now, lick them. Show me how much you crave your submission."

Harold hesitated for a moment, his mind racing with thoughts of what he was doing. But as he felt Dr. Marks' boots against his face, he knew he couldn't resist. He opened his mouth and gently licked the leather, feeling the rough texture against his tongue.

Dr. Marks watched him closely, her expression unreadable. "Good," she repeated, her voice still a mixture of approval and challenge. "Now, swallow your desires and accept your role as my submissive."

Harold felt overwhelmed, both by the surge of submission he was experiencing and by the feeling of being completely under Dr. Marks' control. But as he looked up at her, he knew that he couldn't deny his desires any longer.

"Yes, mistress," he whispered, his voice trembling with submission.

Dr. Marks smiled, a wicked glint in her eye. "

Dr. Marks' tall black leather boots glistened in the light, reaching up to her thighs and dominating Harold's vision. Her eyes held a mischievous glint as she leaned closer to him.

The rich scent of leather filled Harold's nostrils as he knelt before Dr. Marks' boots. It was both comforting and arousing.

As instructed, Harold hesitantly licked the boots, feeling the rough texture against his tongue. The taste was unlike anything he had experienced before, both foreign and enticing.

The sound of Dr. Marks' voice was like honey, tempting and alluring. As she gave him commands,

Dr. Marks' boots were a symbol of power and dominance, their gleaming leather reflecting the flicker of control she held over Harold's desires. As she watched him on his knees, submitting to her every command, she knew he was hers completely and she relished in it.

It was at that moment that Harold realized he had found what he had been searching for all along - a true sense of submission and connection to someone else's dominance. The experience with Dr. Marks was more than just a therapy session; it was a breakthrough that would forever change the way he viewed himself and his relationship with his wife.

Through his submission to Dr. Marks, Harold discovered a new side of himself that he had never known existed. He found that he was capable of being fully submissive and that it was a deeply satisfying experience both physically and emotionally.

In the weeks that followed, Harold and Dr. Marks continued their sessions, exploring his submission in new and exciting ways. She taught him to serve her in ways he never thought possible, and he reveled in the opportunity to worship her in such a submissive role.

As Harold's relationship with Dr. Marks deepened, he began to think about how he could apply these lessons to his marriage. He knew that his wife would be surprised by his newfound submission, but he also knew that she would appreciate the effort he was making to improve their relationship.

Harold had covered one of her boots with his spittle and was starting on the other one when she stopped him. "That is enough for today, Harold. If you want to finish licking my boots the next time that I see you, you will obey me now. Do you understand me?"

"Yes, mistress, I will do anything you tell me to do," Harold replied submissively.

"Here is what I demand that you do," the stern voice commanded. The words cut through the air like a blade, leaving no room for argument or hesitation. "You will go home and tell Susan how sorry you are for not sharing her experience with Master Alexander. You will beg her forgiveness for not staying and witnessing her submission." Cold sweat dripped down his brow as he imagined the look of disappointment on his partner's face. "You will tell her how excited that you became thinking of what Master Alexander was doing to her. You will admit that you masturbated as you fantasized about his cock entering her, stretching her and causing her to moan with pleasure." The weight of shame settled in his chest as he relived the forbidden thoughts that had consumed him. He could almost feel the flames of guilt lapping at his conscience, threatening to consume him whole. But it was what had been demanded of him, and he knew he had no choice but to obey.

Chapter Eleven – Harold Confesses to Susan

Harold was surprised when he entered the house to find his wife sitting in a large armchair wearing high black leather boots, even more alluring than the pair that Dr. Marks was wearing. She looked up as he walked into the room, a smile coming to her face.

Harold's mind was racing as he tried to figure out how to approach his wife with the truth. His heart ached with guilt and he longed to confess everything, but fear held him back.

"Is everything okay, Harold? You seem distracted," Susan noticed, breaking through his thoughts.

He forced a smile and shook his head, trying to hide the turmoil inside. "I just need to talk to you about something."

"Of course, what is it?" Susan replied, her tone warm and inviting.

Harold grabbed a chair and sat nervously in front of her. He couldn't help but feel guilty for not following Doctor Marks' orders to be on his knees, but how could he explain that to Susan without revealing the truth?

Her gaze softened as she leaned towards him. "Are you comfortable sitting like that?" she asked, her concern evident in her voice.

Harold's gaze fell to the ground as he struggled with his conflicting desires - to tell her everything or shield her from the inevitable pain. "I-I'm fine... I just need to tell you something important," he stammered, his voice wavering with uncertainty.

Susan's eyes narrowed slightly as she studied him, trying to decipher his hidden thoughts. "Is it about your session with Doctor Marks?" she asked calmly, her voice belying the turmoil she felt inside.

Harold blinked rapidly, his throat tight with nervousness. "How did you know about that?" he asked, surprised.

"It doesn't matter how I know. What matters is that you have been hiding things from me, things that I have a right to know," Susan replied firmly.

"I am deeply sorry for not being honest with you, Susan. I want to make it right now by telling you the truth. But I fear that you will hate me once you know my secret," Harold confessed, his heart racing in anticipation of her reaction.

"I think you might be more comfortable on your knees," she said seductively, causing Harold's eyebrows to shoot up in surprise.

He wondered if she had spoken to Dr. Marks after he left the session. Fear gripped him as he asked cautiously, "How much does Dr. Marks know? How much has she told you?"

Susan's eyes met Harold's with a mix of curiosity and concern. "I don't think it matters how much Dr. Marks knows or what she has told me. What matters is that you have been dishonest with me, and that is unacceptable."

Harold felt the weight of her words settle on his shoulders. He could see the anger and disappointment in her eyes, and it was like a physical blow to his chest. "I know that I have been dishonest with you, and I am deeply sorry. I didn't know how to tell you the truth without hurting you more," he admitted.

"Then tell me now, Harold. Let everything out and be done with it."

"I...I'm sorry for leaving you alone with Master Alexander," Harold's voice faltered as he spoke.

"Why? Do you think it would have made a difference if you had stayed?" She shot back, her gaze piercing into him.

"I...no, I don't. I understand why you needed to submit, and I should have been there to support you."

She uncrossed her legs and let her boot graze his cheek lightly. "Tell me, Harold. Tell me what you did while I was with Master Alexander. How did it make you feel?"

Harold felt a twinge of betrayal, knowing that Dr. Marks must have told her everything. But then he realized that maybe it was for the best - she needed to know all the dark details of that day. And he couldn't deny his conflicted feelings about it all.

"I...I can't," Harold stammered, feeling a wave of guilt wash over him.

"Why not, Harold? Is it because of what you did? Or because of how you felt?" Susan inquired, her voice low and seductive.

Gulping, Harold's eyes dropped to the ground. "Both... I... I just can't."

Susan's lips curled into a smirk. "Well, if you want to make things right, you'll have to tell me everything. And I expect you to be honest - no holds barred."

Swallowing hard, Harold took a deep breath. "I... I was jealous. Seeing you submit to Master Alexander... it made me feel... powerless."

"Go on, get it all out," she demanded. "What did you do when you left me there? Did you think about what we must have been doing? Did it arouse you knowing that another man was fucking your wife?"

"You obviously already know that it did. You must also know that I went into our bedroom, stripped off my clothes, and masturbated fantasizing that I was there watching him take you. I could almost hear you moan with pleasure. I could imagine that you were begging him to fuck you deeper. Tell me, did he wear a condom?"

I never even thought to ask him. The anticipation of skin on skin, the heat of his body pressed against mine and the primal pleasure of his release deep inside me was all I wanted. In fact, I wished I wasn't on birth control so his seed could find its way into my fertile womb. How does that make you feel, Harold? Do you still regret not being there, knowing that he gave me more than just physical pleasure? He took a piece of my heart reserved only for you and claimed it as his own. And to answer your next question, yes, I plan on doing it again, with or without you by my side. Although I must admit, I prefer it if you were there to witness it all. To see how he makes me feel, the pleasure he evokes from my very core. To understand that he can do things to me that you never could. That I will willingly do for him what I would never do for you.

He couldn't help but feel an odd mix of jealousy and arousal at her words. His erection was throbbing under his pants, but he also felt a sense of betrayal and sadness.

"Do you want me to tell you more about what happened? What he did to me?" she asked, her voice dripping with pleasure.

For a moment, Harold considered the prospect of learning every detail, of trying to make sense of the twisted desires that he felt. But then he realized that he could never truly understand and that he didn't want to.

In a quiet tone barely above a whisper, he expressed, "No, I believe I comprehend."

"Very well. Let's transition to a less distressing subject. Such as my profound adoration for you being my cuckold, Harold. Have you any idea the extent of my delight in surrendering to another man's dominance?" Susan provocatively inquired.

A swirl of jealousy and arousal intertwined within Harold, acknowledging his inability to compete with Susan's vivid fantasies. Despite the turmoil, his love for her remained unwavering as he couldn't envision life without her.

Lost in conflicting emotions, Harold confessed to Susan, "I am torn, unsure of how to navigate this emotional turbulence. My love for you is undeniable, yet the jealousy and anguish persist. How do we proceed from here?"

Susan's seductive whispers caressed his ear, laden with dark desires. "This consuming intensity within you only adds to the allure," she uttered softly, her touch igniting fiery sensations across his skin.

With a sense of submission enveloping him, Harold accepted the business card Susan extended to him. Ready to plead and submit to Master Alexander's will, all in pursuit of bearing witness to his own wife's domination.

As Harold stared at the business card in his hand, a mix of anticipation and trepidation washed over him. The thought of entering this unknown world of dominance and submission both thrilled and frightened him. Susan's seductive gaze beckoned him to take the next step, to surrender fully to her desires.

Taking a deep breath to steady himself, Harold made a decision. He would embark on this journey with Susan, trusting in their love to guide them through uncharted waters. With a newfound sense of resolve, he turned to her and nodded, silently affirming his willingness to explore this new dynamic in their relationship.

Susan's eyes sparkled with delight as she led Harold towards a path paved with challenges and revelations. Together, they would navigate the complexities of power dynamics and unearth hidden depths within themselves. And as they ventured into the realm of Master Alexander's domain, they did so not as master and submissive, but as partners bound by an unbreakable bond of trust and devotion.

At that moment, Harold understood that their love was not limited by conventional boundaries but thrived in the freedom to explore every facet of their desires. And as they stepped into the unknown, hand in hand, he knew that no matter where their journey led them, they would face it together, united in their shared passion and unwavering commitment to each other

Chapter Twelve The Unveiling of Desires

Harold's voice shook with desperation as he pleaded with Master Alexander to let him witness his wife's next session. He promised to do anything, no matter how degrading or painful.

"And yet, I have doubts about your loyalty after your behavior last time," Master Alexander replied coldly. "If you truly want to prove yourself, would you consent to be tied up and placed on a stool, completely helpless and unable to interfere in any way?" The image of being restrained and forced to watch filled Harold with dread, but he knew he had no choice if he wanted to regain Master Alexander's trust.

"Yes, I will agree to that and to any other condition that you may impose upon me, Sir," Harold said, swallowing hard. His voice trembled with the effort of his submission.

"Very well," Master Alexander replied, his voice hard and unyielding. "Meet me at my place at eight o'clock sharp tomorrow night, and bring your wife with you. I will inform you of your obligations when you arrive."

With that, Master Alexander hung up the phone, leaving Harold to stew in his anxiety and distress. He knew that the next few days would be fraught with tension, but he also knew that he had to follow through with his promise if he hoped to regain his wife's trust.

As the day approached, Harold began to devise a plan to show Master Alexander his loyalty and commitment. He knew that he had to prove himself, and he was willing to do whatever it took.

When the night finally arrived, Harold and Susan showed up promptly at eight o'clock sharp. As they entered Master Alexander's dungeon, they were greeted by an intense atmosphere of anticipation and desire.

The room was a sensuous labyrinth, bathed in the warm glow of dimmed lights. The atmosphere hung heavy with an intoxicating blend of desire and excitement, filled with the musky scent of masculinity and the tantalizing aroma of worn leather. Harold and Susan stepped into Master Alexander's realm, their hearts hammering wildly against their ribcages as they were swallowed by this world of raw dominance.

Alexander, a towering figure dressed in authoritative black, commanded the room with an aura that set their pulses racing. "Undress," his voice echoed through the room, reverberating off the walls, a command laced with as much seduction as an assertion.

Susan obeyed, shedding her clothing layer by layer, until she stood before him in all her bare vulnerability. Her body glowed under the soft lighting, her curves whispering promises of pleasure yet to be explored.

Harold watched on from the sidelines, his shoulders bowed with a cocktail of emotions - jealousy gnawed at him as he watched Alexander's predatory gaze consume his wife's exposed form. Yet, within him stirred a strange heat, as embers fanned to life by Susan's submissive display.

With a calculated grace, Alexander moved towards Harold and bound him securely to a stool. A sense of helpless thrill sparked within Harold at the act of bondage – his wrists and ankles strained against the ropes but there was no pain; instead, it elicited an anticipatory shiver that ran down his spine.

As Alexander turned his attention back to Susan, Harold could do nothing but watch from his captive position. He observed as Alexander traced slow circles on Susan's flushed skin, each touch setting her body on fire. She quivered beneath his skilled hands while soft gasps escaped her lips, echoing through the room like symphonic cries of pleasure.

Harold found himself entranced by this erotic spectacle playing out before him. His veins pulsed with a mix of emotions - fear, jealousy, and a strange, alarming arousal. Alexander's mastery over Susan was undeniable, his fingers coaxing sinful moans from her lips - each touch akin to a maestro drawing notes of pleasure from his instrument.

As the room reverberated with their symphony of desire, Harold found himself spiraling into a whirlpool of emotions. His mind was a battlefield where jealousy and dark desire waged war. Every shudder, every whimper that escaped Susan twisted him inside out. Yet this was what she craved, what she sought.

Thus, in the intoxicating dance of eroticism choreographed by Master Alexander, Harold watched on; his heart pounding in sync with the rhythm of his wife's raw passion ignited by another man - a turbulent blend of yearning and surrender painting vivid strokes across the canvas of his psyche.

Master Alexander then guided Susan to lie on her back on a padded bench; her head hanging off one end and her derriere exposed at the other. As he commanded her to spread her legs as wide as possible, he produced lengths of rope from his pocket. Her ankles were securely tied to poles on either side of the bench. Now, completely at the mercy of her Master's whims, Susan's arousal glistened on the blonde tendrils guarding her femininity. The scent of her musk hung heavily in the air or perhaps it was just Harold's imagination flirting with his senses.

With skilled hands, Alexander then secured a soft leather belt under Susan's back and fastened it with a large buckle – each movement heightening her sense of vulnerability. Her hands were then bound to rings on either side of the belt. As she lay there completely surrendered to her Master's desires, anticipation sparked within her, making her nipples harden at the thought of his thick member invading her.

As Alexander stood over Susan in all his naked glory – muscles sculpted to perfection from hours spent at the gym, his phallus hung between his legs like a symbol of raw masculinity. Harold watched on from the sidelines, bewitched and bewildered at this display of dominance. As Alexander guided his member into Susan's waiting mouth, Harold was gripped by envy, excitement, and a strange sense of arousal.

"Has she ever sucked your cock, Harold"? Master Alexander asked him. Harold didn't answer and Master Alexander asked the same question of Susan.

"No, I have never had a cock in my mouth. I would have done that for Harold but he never asked me."

Eyes holding onto each other's gazes, Alexander began to gently tease Susan's virgin mouth with the velvety tip of his substantial length. She gasped audibly then - the first tease of wet warmth enveloping him invitingly and opening doors to a depth unseen before. Her eyes widened at this new invasion, cheeks hollowed out beautifully as she attempted to adapt her innocence to accept him completely.

The sight of Susan's lips wrapped tight around Alexander's girth stirred a cocktail of envy and arousal within Harold. If it weren't for the leather cuffs binding his hands, they would have instinctively mirrored the rhythm of pleasure unfolding before his eyes. His cock was rock hard and he desperately wanted to touch it, to caress it, to bring himself to an orgasm he knew he had never experienced before.

A soft moan filled the room as Master Alexander teased his engorged tip back and forth across her swollen lips. Harold didn't realize that the sound had come from his mouth. "Open for me, slut," came the masterful command from Alexander's lips. Harold watched in awe as Susan obediently widened her mouth further, accommodating more of Alexander than he thought possible. Her delicate features contorted in pleasurable ecstasy while her tongue made love to the shaft's thick length- a sight that aroused and incited jealousy in equal measures in Harold.

The air hung heavy with an intoxicating blend of sweat-infused lust and the rich leather scent from restraining straps binding Harold in the seductively submissive position. A faint whiff of Susan's perfume added a sweet contrast to the raw, animalistic ambiance they were all enveloped in.

Gagging slightly as Alexander breached her throat's depths, Susan was guided to breathe through her nose and calm her heated mind. As she succumbed to the overwhelming pleasure coursing through her body, he held her head firmly in place, rhythmically pushing deeper into her inviting warmth. Moans filled the room, overlaid with a hint of gagging - sounds that perfectly complemented the scent of her arousal wafting through the air.

At this sight, Harold felt an odd amalgamation of emotions: envy, desire, and even a strange sense of pride seeing his wife expertly pleasuring another man in such an erotic manner. He began imagining what it would feel like to have Susan's inviting mouth around him.

With wrists bound in soft restraints, Susan was left helpless to touch herself even as intensity spiked within her writhing form under Alexander's skillful control. Gasps turned into hushed whimpering cries while Harold found himself holding onto his breath, craving to hear more.

Alexander finally pulled away from Susan's welcoming depths, leaving both men aching for more. Sensations still lingered on Susan's lips well after Alexander had retreated. The glistening tip of his virile member rubbed against them continuously eliciting soft groans from Susan each time. Her obedience shone brightly when she allowed Alexander back inside without hesitation; the cock was not distasteful but rather surprisingly pleasant. She tried massaging it with her tongue despite how much it stretched out her cheeks - offering a feast for Harold's eyes during their salacious exchange.

Master Alexader pushed forward slowly allowing Susan time to prepare for the assault on her throat that was coming. She sucked in as hard as she could hoping to bring a little of his precum into her mouth.

The air between them crackled with tension as Susan continued to worship Master Alexander's cock with her mouth, the sucking and moaning filling the room.

Harold could feel his desire rising, imagining the warm, wet sensation of his wife's mouth around him. The thought made his cock twitch in response. He mentally begged her to look at him, to let him see the pleasure she was giving to this other man.

Susan's eyes met Harold's for a brief moment, her gaze a mixture of guilt and lust before returning her focus to Alexander's swollen member in her mouth. Harold's heart thumped painfully in his chest, the sight both arousing and humiliating him. He felt like he was losing control like this man had taken something precious from him.

Master Alexander continued to thrust in and out of Susan's mouth, the rhythm becoming faster and more forceful. Susan's gag reflex triggered with each deep throat, her moans, and gasps echoing in the now steamy room. Harold could imagine the taste of his cock in her mouth, the sensation of her tongue swirling around his shaft. The fantasy sent a jolt of lust through him, his tied hands throbbing with the desire to touch himself.

Harold's eyes widened in shock as he watched Master Alexander groan loudly, his hips thrust forward and releasing his seed into Susan's mouth. The expression on Susan's face was one of submission and adoration, her eyes closed and lips parted as she took in her Master's release. Master Alexander's glistening cock and the sight of him wiping some of the mess off Susan's chin with his finger sent a rush of emotions through Harold.

As Alexander's cum filled Susan's mouth, she choked and gagged on the thick liquid, the taste of salt and bitterness overwhelming her taste buds. Harold could almost taste it himself, imagining the forbidden act before him.

And then Master Alexander pulled back his thick cock dripping with Susan's juices and his cum. A small amount of that mixture fell on Susan's chin. Alexander reached out with his fingers and wiped that morsel off onto his fingers. Instead of offering it to Susan, he walked over holding his cum covered fingers to Harold's lips. Although Harold was more humiliated than he had ever been in his life he opened allowing those fingers into his mouth.

"Now, suck it clean, slave," he told Harold.

And Harold obeyed. Seeing this Susan smiled glad to see that her husband was also to become a slave to her Master.

Susan's body writhed beneath Alexander in wild abandon, the sensations threatening to consume her. The mixture of pain and pleasure heightened her senses, making every touch feel like bolts of electricity coursing through her veins.

That wasn't part of Master Alexander's plan. He walked back to the bench where Susan was tied, stepped between her legs, and touched the tip of his cock to her opening. He began rubbing it up and down her wet slit, causing her to moan and beg for him to fuck her.

Harold watched with a mix of disgust and fascination as the man's previously rigid member now hung limp and lifeless. He assumed that Master Alexander would finally release his captives, allowing them to clean up from the ordeal. But instead, he had other plans.

Stepping over to where Susan was securely tied to the bench, he positioned himself between her spread legs and gently prodded at her entrance with his flaccid shaft. She moaned and squirmed beneath him, her wetness coating his member as he rubbed it against her sensitive folds. With each touch to her throbbing clit, she begged for him to take her, a desperate plea for release.

Harold could hardly believe it as he watched the man's well-spent cock begin to grow again. With each stroke up and down Susan's slick slit, it grew harder until the man had to step back to avoid his shaft entering his captive slave.

Harold couldn't believe what he was witnessing: Alexander's once limply spent cock began hardening again at the sight and sounds of Susan's unabashed longing. Every stroke up and down her slick slit seemed to breathe life back into his manhood, making him a force to be reckoned with once more.

The power dynamics in the room had shifted, as had the erotic energy. It was no longer about humiliation but about dominance, submission, and arousal beyond words.

The sound of Susan begging seemed to excite Master Alexander even more. "I love to hear you beg, slut. Tell Harold what you think of my cock."

He reached between their bodies, spreading her cunt lips with two fingers of his left hand. With his right, he positioned the head of his now blood-engorged cock to her entrance and pushed forward, his hips straining with the effort because of how tight Susan's hole was.

"Tell him, slut," Alexander demanded.

"Yes, Master," she began. "Harold, can you see what he is doing to me? Do you understand that he is stretching me much further than your pencil dick ever could? He is ruining me for you, husband. Oh God, I love his cock. No, that isn't true, I worship his cock."

Alexander was pleased with Susan's elocution and pressed forward, causing Susan to cry out with pain. "Do you want me to stop, slut?" he asked her.

"God no, Master, I want you to hurt me. Go deeper, into my womb if you can. I can feel the tip of your cock trying to spread the entrance even now."

Alexander pushed forward with all his might, but the ring surrounding the opening of Susan's womb was too tight. With a cruel grin, he pulled out and delivered a sharp slap across Susan's face. "You're not trying hard enough," he sneered. "Let's see if we can't loosen you up a bit."

With that, he reached for a nearby metal dildo with a tapered point. He showed it to her eliciting a gasp as she realized what he was going to do. Spreading her cunt lips he pushed the dildo inside of her guiding it to the tight ring separating her cunt from her womb. "Tell me when you feel it pushing against your womb opening, slut," he demanded.

"You are there now, Master, push it in." She cried out when Master Alexander obeyed and pushed the hard dildo inside of her womb. He began to move it back and forth trying to widen the entrance for when he again fucked his slave.

Susan writhed in pleasure and pain as the dildo filled her womb, her body betraying her every desire with each thrust. Harold watched in horror and arousal, unable to take his eyes off the scene unfolding before him. He felt a surge of desire for his wife, a longing to be the one to pleasure her, to give her what she craved.

Master Alexander quickly pulled the dildo from Susan and tossed it aside. He positioned his cock to her opening and thrust forward with all his might. He was rewarded when he felt the head of his cock enter her womb. He held it there reveling in hearing her cries of pain. He could feel his orgasm starting and he moved in and out not enough to pull his cock from her womb but just enough to cause friction to his tender excited flesh.

With a final thrust, he buried himself in her one last time; plunging deep beyond the gates of fleshly paradise and marking her as his own forever. The room echoed with cries of release as Alexander flooded her womb with his hot seed, each spurt further claiming Susan as his slave.

Chapter Thirteen-New Experiences

Susan had been released from her night of pleasure with Master Alexander. As she lay beside him in his luxurious king-sized bed, she couldn't help but smile contentedly at her new station in life. Master Alexander had treated her with such tenderness and passion during their intimate moments together, making love to her instead of simply taking her like before. She was filled with a sense of bliss and gratitude as she drifted off to sleep beside him. When they had both enjoyed their orgasms, Master Alexander pulled Susan into his arms, lowering his mouth to hers, and allowed her to suck on his tongue. Susan moaned with pleasure hoping that she could get her Master hard and ready to make love to her again, but that didn't happen. "You need to get some sleep, little one, Alexander crooned to her. Tomorrow will be very busy and filled with more new and exciting challenges for you to accomplish.

You did so well today, I hope that you enjoyed it as much as I did."

"I have never spent a more enjoyable day in my life. Thank you so much, I love you."

Alexander was a little surprised at Susan's words. He had expected that she would be grateful for the experience and the newfound freedom, but perhaps he had underestimated the depth of her feelings for him.

He could not reciprocate her declaration of love. Love was a foreign concept to him when it came to her. He found satisfaction in her gradual surrender to his commands and eagerly anticipated the day he could unleash his sadistic desires upon her. Seeing her degrade and humiliate the man she was married to only added to his twisted enjoyment. And yet, he still craved more - the thought of seeing her physically harm the man sent shivers of anticipation down his spine, fueling his thirst for sadistic pleasure. "I will open new worlds to you, little one. What we have done so far is just the tip of the iceberg."

Susan nodded, her eyes shining with tears. "I know, Master. You have already given me so much. I just want to make sure that you know how much I appreciate it."

Alexander smiled and pulled her into a deep, lingering kiss. He knew that they would have many more challenging days and nights ahead of them, but for now, he was content to bask in the warmth of Susan's love and the knowledge that he had found something truly special in her.

They shared a shower before going downstairs to release Harold from his bondage.

As Harold lay crumpled on the floor, writhing in pain, Susan couldn't help but feel a twisted sense of satisfaction. She reveled in his misery, knowing that she was the cause of his suffering. Master Alexander had awakened something dark within her, a hunger for control and domination that she never knew existed.

As they watched Harold in his agony, Susan's heart raced with excitement. She couldn't wait to see the look of terror on his face as he realized the depths of her betrayal. But Master Alexander's plans for Susan went far beyond mere humiliation. He had glimpsed the darkness within her, and he intended to nurture it, to bring it to the forefront and revel in its power. He would push her to her limits, forcing her to confront her deepest fears and desires. And Susan, trapped in the thrall of his dominance, would follow him willingly into the abyss.

Master Alexander's sinister intentions for Susan transcended mere humiliation. He had peered into the depths of her soul, recognizing the shadows that lurked within, and he planned to cultivate them, to unleash their formidable force. His goal was to test her boundaries relentlessly, compelling her to face her most profound fears and longings head-on. Ensnared in the grip of his command, Susan would willingly tread alongside him into the unfathomable darkness.

A light breakfast was prepared with cold efficiency, a silent reminder of his place in this household. Susan enjoyed her meal while ignoring her pathetic husband, but she made sure to set out a metal dish filled with warm tap water on the floor for him. Harold's stomach growled at the sight, but he knew better than to ask for food.

With aching limbs, Harold crawled to the bowl and reached out with trembling hands to pick it up and drink from it like an animal. But before he could even touch it, Susan swooped in like a bird of prey and snatched the bowl away. With a swift kick of her booted foot, she pushed Harold flat onto the floor and twisted his arms behind his back in a painful hold. Master Alexander watched with amusement as he picked up a pair of handcuffs and secured Harold's hands behind him.

Susan's voice dripped with venom as she purred, "That's better, my dear husband. Now you can get your drink like the dog that you truly are." Harold hung his head in shame, feeling nothing but utter humiliation and degradation at the hands of his wife and her lover.

Harold inched forward on his belly until his mouth could reach the bowl. His stomach rolled slightly at the gross taste of the warm chlorine-laced water as he sucked a mouthful.

As Harold lapped up the disgusting water, Alexander could see the terror in his eyes. He knew that he was breaking Harold, both physically and mentally. He watched as Susan taunted her husband, her face twisted with sadistic delight. This was the kind of control and domination that he had been looking for in her.

He had known from the start that Susan was submissive by nature, but now he saw that there was something darker, something more dangerous hidden within her. He made a mental note to explore this dark side of her in the coming days.

As Harold finished drinking, Susan released him from the painful hold on his arms and kicked him away, back to his place on the floor. She gestured for him to crawl toward her, and Harold, humiliated and defeated, obeyed.

Susan and Alexanders at down at the table, sharing a light breakfast. Harold, however, was relegated to staying on his knees beside Susan's booted feet. He had learned this was his place from this day forward.

Finally allowed to stand, Harold stumbled towards the dungeon shower, his muscles screaming in protest from the previous night's torment. The frigid water pounded against his bruised skin, sending shards of icy pain through his already battered body. It was as if the very temperature served as a reminder of his insignificance.

Drying himself off with the same towel that once caressed Susan's and Master Alexander's bodies, Harold couldn't help but feel an overwhelming sense of degradation. The fabric seemed to mock him, whispering cruel reminders of his place in this perverse hierarchy.

Desperately hoping for a shred of dignity, Harold asked for his clothes. But Susan only smiled her expression a haunting mix of sadism and control. With a wicked flourish, she handed him a pair of bright red panties, relishing in the humiliation it would bring.

Protesting weakly, Harold's voice trembled as he dared to challenge Susan's domination. But her response was swift and cutting, her words laced with venomous authority. She reminded him, with a chilling certainty, that he was no longer a man but a pawn in their twisted game.

Susan watched with pleasure as her husband inched the panties up his legs and over his hips. "Perhaps I will allow you to wear a bra sometime but not now. If you decide that you would like me to completely feminize you, you can remove all your body hair and I will consider it. For today here is a skirt, blouse, and a pair of white women's sandals. But, don't worry unlike me you will not have to walk home. Of course, I suppose drivers in high-rise vehicles will be able to see how you are dressed. If you are lucky some guy might even ask you for a date.

The darkness grew thicker as Harold reluctantly donned the panties, feeling his very identity slipping away under their unrelenting torment. The room pulsated with sinister energy as Susan and Master

Alexander reveled in their power over him, fueled by the exhilaration of breaking a soul beyond repair.

And so, the nightmare continued, the tendrils of sadism wrapping tighter around Harold's shattered spirit. With each passing moment, he descended further into the depths of their depravity, trapped in an inferno of darkness from which there seemed to be no escape.

Harold made his way to the dungeon door and without looking back he walked outside and headed to his car.

It was only a few minutes later when his wife walked out the door. He gasped as he realized that all she had on was her lingerie and boots.

Harold followed her as she stepped out into the busy street and started her trek toward her home 5 miles away. She was carrying two black bags one in each hand. Harold could not know that Alexander had ordered her to carry the bags so that she would not try to cover any section of her body should someone confront her.

As Susan walked away, Harold couldn't help but feel a strange mix of emotions. On one hand, he was disgusted by her nakedness and humiliated by his submissiveness. On the other hand, there was a strange sense of arousal, a curiosity that gnawed at him, daring him to explore this new world of dominance and submission.

He followed her from a distance, trying to make sense of it all. The more he watched, the more he felt his resolve weakening. The more he resisted, the more his rebellious side seemed to take over.

He found himself wondering what it would be like to be the one in charge, to exert the same level of control over Susan that Alexander had over him. What would it be like to see the look of terror on her face, to hear her screams of pain and pleasure?

Finally, he pulled his car alongside his wife opened the passenger door, and told her to get in. Susan's face contorted in anger.

"When are you going to learn that you don't make decisions for me? My Master ordered me to walk the five miles to our house and I am going to do that. You are welcome to follow if you want but only if you do it on foot so that everyone can see your skirt, blouse, and pretty sandals."

Harold just shook his head, closed the door, and drove away. He looked back with regret knowing that the beautiful woman behind him no longer belonged to him.

Susan felt shame as she walked along the busy street drawing stares from both men and women, catcalls from some, and obscenities from others. Several times men would roll down their windows and yell "Do you want to fuck" before driving away. Once a police car went speeding by and she was afraid that he would turn around and arrest her for indecent exposure but he was running his lights in a hurry to get to the scene of an accident or perhaps a crime.

She had gone about halfway the distance to her home when a large limousine pulled up alongside her and stopped. The door opened and a very large black man in a white suit got out and approached her.

"What are you doing working my territory, slut?" he asked in a loud demanding voice.

The man's voice boomed, cutting through the quiet of the street. "What are you doing working my territory, slut?" His heavy footsteps approached Susan, who was frozen in fear.

"I am sorry sir," she stammered, lowering her gaze. "I am not working anyone's territory. I am just on my way home."

A sneer crossed the man's face as he eyed her up and down. "Look Whore, I wasn't born yesterday. No white slut would be walking along this street in that state of undress if she wasn't looking for a John." He gestured to her revealing outfit and the bags she carried. "What have you got in those bags, bitch?"

Susan trembled under his glare. "I am not sure, sir. My Master just ordered me to carry them. He didn't say what was in them. He did say that I was not to open them until I arrived at my house."

The man raised an eyebrow, intrigued by her mention of a Master. "Who is this man you refer to as your Master?" he asked.

"I only know of him by the designation of Master Alexander," Susan replied timidly. "Perhaps you might be familiar with him."

The man's demeanor changed immediately upon hearing the name Master Alexander. He was all too familiar with the powerful figure and knew better than to mess with one of his slaves. "Get in," he said, offering her a ride. "It isn't safe for you to be out here alone and nearly naked. The next man that stops might not be as friendly as I am."

Susan considered the offer for just a few seconds but then she knew that she belonged to Master Alexander and if he wanted her to do this, she would obey.

"Thank you again, sir, but I must decline your generous offer. I can't disobey my Master no matter how much danger I might face."

"That is admirable of you. If you weren't Alexander's slave I would force you to go with me and I would make a ton of money by pimping you out. Here is my card," he said and pushed the small oblong piece of paper into her bra. "Anyone gives you any trouble, give them the card. It even works with most cops."

Susan thanked the man as he got back in his car and it pulled away from the curb.

She hadn't gone more than another quarter of a mile when another car pulled up and stopped beside her. The driver rolled down the window. "Susan, what in the world are you doing on the street nearly naked?'

Susan looked at the man, her minister at the local church.

"Oh, hello, Paster. I just felt like going for a walk this morning.

Susan was mortified, but she knew better than to lie to him. Pastor Johnson had always been a kind man, and she knew that he wouldn't judge her too harshly for her current situation.

"Well, if you need a ride home or anything, I'm more than happy to help," he offered, concern etching his face.

"Thank you that is so kind of you to offer, but I only have a short way to go and the sun feels so good this morning."

"Susan you do realize that you are nearly naked, don't you."

"Oh, I suppose that some might view my attire in that light, but would you think the same thing of a woman wearing a two-piece bathing suit?"

"Well, I think there is a bit of a difference," he admitted, "but even so, I wouldn't want you to put yourself in any danger."

"I appreciate your concern, Pastor. I'll be fine. Thank you."

The man shook his head in wonderment. Then he rolled up his window, started his car, and drove away thinking that there might be a sermon in this situation come the following Sunday.

Susan continued on her way, feeling both embarrassed and intrigued by the attention she was receiving. As she walked, she couldn't help but think about how her life had changed, and how deep she had gone into her submission to Master Alexander. It was a strange and intoxicating feeling, and she found herself both loving and fearing it at the same time. Her humiliation grew as she imagined what the Minister would tell his wife and close friends.

Susan entered the street where she lived and was mortified to see that most of her neighbors were outside either doing yard work, washing their cars, or just enjoying the day.

One particular neighbor, an old widow with a curious gaze and a knack for gossip, couldn't help but stare at Susan's exposed body as she walked past her house. The old woman's eyes widened in shock, her mouth agape. She rushed inside to get her phone so that she could take a picture of her seemingly prim and proper neighbor. She couldn't help thinking of all the wonderful gossip that she could share with other people that both she and Susan knew.

Susan continued her walk, trying to ignore the stares and whispers from her neighbors. She had never felt so exposed and vulnerable in her life. As she approached her house, she saw her husband Harold standing at the door, looking just as shocked and embarrassed as she was.

"Well, are you happy now that the entire neighborhood has seen you parading around like Lady Godiva?'

Susan smiled at him, suddenly glad that she had done this for her Master. Harold was more mortified that the neighbors had seen her in her lingerie than she was. "Don't be ridiculous. Lady Godiva was naked not wearing lingerie and she was riding a horse. But, now that you mention it, I do know a friend who has a stable. I am sure she would let me borrow a horse if I told her what I wanted to do with it."

"When did you become such a bitch?" Harold asked her.

"I have always been a bitch, dear husband, I just didn't know it before I met Master Alexander. I noticed that you haven't bothered to remove your body hair as I instructed. If you want to worship these boots the way you worshipped Dr. Marks' boots you will get with the program.

As Harold stood there, his mind whirled with confusion and desire. His wife's suggestion of boot worship seemed to awaken something deep within him, but he couldn't shake the humiliation he felt from her actions earlier.

"Get inside and clean yourself up," he eventually snapped, not knowing how else to respond.

Susan smiled and walked past him, leaving him standing on the front porch. Inside, she went straight to the shower to wash away the remnants of her morning walk. Once clean, she put on a short leather skirt a white blouse, and her boots and waited for Harold to come to her.

When he finally did, she was standing in the bedroom, her legs slightly spread and her hands on her hips. "So, my dear husband, what do you decide? Will you worship these boots, or will I shame you even more in front of our neighbors?"

Harold looked at her, his eyes filled with a mix of lust and anger. He knew that she had broken him in more ways than one, and yet he could not deny the desire that gripped him at her feet.

He dropped to his knees, his hands shaking slightly as he reached out to touch her boots. The smooth leather felt like a command to him - to submit to her, to obey her every wish.

As Harold's tongue gently brushed against the polished surface of her boots, Susan smirked. She had seen Harold's weakness, and she would use it to her advantage.

"Take out your cock wimp, I want to see how hard you get while you are bebasing yourself in front of me."

Susan began laughing as she saw her husband pull his small piece of meat out of his pants. It was as hard as it ever had been in the past, but compared to the magnificent phallus of Master Alexander it looked like a large clit. "Remember watching Master Alexander fucking me with his beautiful cock. Now look down and tell me what you see?"

Harold was drowning in a sea of an unfamiliar, yet powerful, mix of humiliation and excitement as he listened to his wife's commanding voice. He found himself averted from her piercing gaze, only to receive a stinging slap across his face. His surprise wasn't just from the slap itself, but rather the raw and primal reaction it triggered within him. Even in his wildest fantasies, he'd never pictured Susan asserting her dominance over him like this. Now that she had, an intoxicating arousal coursed through him, its potency leaving him staggered.

He stole a glance at his own body, at the visible signs of his arousal slowly subsiding - a fact which seemed to stir an even deeper sense of shame and yet a stronger longing within him.

A silent realization struck him: there was no escape from this predicament. He was completely ensnared by Susan's will. Obediently on his knees now, he leaned forward to submit to her command. His tongue traced the smooth leather of her left boot first, gradually moving to the right one. Each stroke left a warm trail on the cold surface, symbolic of his escalating submission and humiliation.

Susan watched Harold with a wicked smirk curling upon her lips. The sight of his flushed face twisted in shock seemed to bring out even more delight within her.

"That's it, you weakling," she threw an arrogant taunt his way, her velvet voice dripping with supremacy. "Prove your love for these boots of mine. Show me what a willing servant you are for me."

Harold continued on his task, each lick adding another layer to his embarrassment while strangely fueling his exhilaration. Caught in an extraordinarily vulnerable situation like this was something utterly new for him - mortifying and titillating at once.

As he reached the end of Susan's right boot with one final lick, he felt her firm grip on his hair. She tugged it, pulling his head upwards to finally meet her gaze. Her eyes flashed with power and satisfaction as he looked up, painting a vivid picture of the electrifying moment.

Now, tell me what you see. How would you describe your pathetic piece of meat compared to the magnificent cock that my Master possesses?

"My piece of meat is small and weak," Harold muttered shamelessly, his eyes still locked with Susan's. "It doesn't compare to the strength and power of Master Alexander's magnificent cock."

"I am glad that you realize that. It makes it easier for me to tell you that you will never again put that worthless piece of meat inside of me. It should also make it easier for you to accept that I will be fucking Master Alexander as often as he will allow me to. By the way, did you enjoy seeing me such his cock today? You realize that had you asked me to do that for you I would have gladly agreed. But, that opportunity for you has passed and it will never be repeated.

Harold's eyes stayed fixed on the floor, unable to meet Susan's gaze. He felt a shiver run down his spine as she spoke, her voice laced with venomous satisfaction.

"Now, you'll learn your place, Harold. You'll understand that you are nothing but my pathetic little slave, eager to do my bidding."

She paused for a moment, savoring the power that she held over him.

"Tell me, Harold. How does it feel to know that you'll never again experience the warmth of my body? That your pathetic excuse for a cock will never again be welcomed in my presence?"

Harold's shame was absolute, his face burning with humiliation. He couldn't bring himself to speak, to admit the truth of his inadequacy.

"I'll take that as a 'yes,'" Susan sneered, her voice dripping with contempt. "You'll learn to accept your new role, Harold. You'll learn to revel in your degradation, to find pleasure in your humiliation."

She reached down, grabbing a handful of his hair and yanking his head back. He winced in pain but didn't dare to resist.

"You'll learn to love serving me, Harold. To love being my slave. And if you're very, very lucky, I might even allow you to witness my encounters with Master Alexander. To see the magnificent cock that you can never hope to compare to."

She released him, letting him fall back to his knees with a thud. He stayed there, defeated and humiliated, as she walked away.

"Oh, and Harold? I wouldn't get too attached to those clothes. I think it's time for you to learn what it means to be my slave."

And with that, she was gone, leaving him alone in his misery. He knew that he had no choice but to obey, to submit to her will. He was her slave now, and he would do whatever she commanded. Even if it meant stripping naked and waiting for her return, vulnerable and exposed.

He could only hope that one day, he might find a way to regain his dignity, to reclaim his place in the world. But for now, he was nothing but a pathetic, shivering wreck, trembling at the mercy of his cruel and sadistic wife.

Harold's desire surged within him, his blood-engorged cock begging for attention. The irresistible urge to stroke it to completion danced at the edge of his restraint. Yet, beneath it all, a deeper longing stirred - a craving for his wife to seize control, to command his orgasms and confine him in a cruel chastity cage. Perhaps one adorned with needles, a ruthless reminder training him never to achieve an erection again.

Chapter Fourteen-Harold's Training Continues

Harold stayed on his knees for what seemed like hours, hoping that Susan would come back and tell him what she wanted him to become. His heart beat faster, wondering if Susan would turn him into some kind of sissy slave, an obedient servant who would serve her guests at dinner parties. He remembered her saying that she might feminize him and wondered how he would feel wearing a French Maid's uniform and sky-high heels in front of friends and family.

The thought intrigued him but at the same time terrified him. The more he thought about it, the more he wanted Susan to make him into whatever she desired. He didn't care what it was as long as it was her ultimate decision.

Harold's thoughts were interrupted by the sound of the front door opening, signaling Susan's return. His heart raced in anticipation, unsure of what he would be forced to become. Susan walked into the room, her dominance apparent at every step.

"Get up, Harold," she commanded. "It's time for you to learn what you'll be from now on."

Harold hesitated for a moment before obeying, rising shakily to his feet. He was terrified, unsure of what was in store for him, but he knew there was no escape. This was his fate now, and he had to accept it.

She ordered him to strip off his clothes and put on the skirt and blouse that she had given him earlier as well as black sandals.

"Remember I told you that I was going to feminize you and the first step is to go shopping for your female clothing. You do want to do that don't you Harriet?"

This was another surprise for Harold. He hadn't even considered that his wife would give him a feminine name. But deep down it pleased him knowing that his wife was not taking this lightly. He wondered how she would rectify the fact that he had not shaven his body as she had directed. Part of him hoped there might be some punishment involved.

"Yes, Mistress," he replied, swallowing hard. "I will do anything you ask of me."

Susan smiled cruelly, seeing the fear and uncertainty in her captive's eyes. "That's the right attitude, Harriet. Now come along, we have shopping to do."

As they left the house, Harold felt a strange mixture of emotions. Part of him was filled with dread, knowing that this was the beginning of a new life as Susan's plaything. But another part of him was excited, curious about what his wife had in mind for him.

Just then the doorbell rang and Susan demanded that her new slave go and see who was there. Harold gasped in horror as he saw his sister, Monica, standing on the stoop. She was wearing a short leather skirt and black leather pumps with sky-high heels. Her red silk blouse clung to her nylon encased breasts causing the material to bulge out.

"Susan told me that you had turned into a god damned queer, but I didn't believe it until right now.

Harold's heart raced as he tried to come up with a response, but his words caught in his throat. The woman standing in front of him was breathtaking, with long, flowing hair and piercing blue eyes. She brushed past him, still shaking her head in disbelief at what she had just seen. As she entered the living room, Susan stood to greet her, radiating confidence and beauty.

Harold couldn't help but notice how stunning both women were, wondering why he had never noticed this about his sister before. He felt a twinge of jealousy at their effortless charm and grace.

Susan spoke up, breaking the tense silence. "I need Harriet here to buy some feminine garments for herself so that she will stop taking mine. Would you mind taking him to the mall and witnessing him as he buys several sets of bras and panties, as well as garters and stockings? And perhaps take him to a shoe store and have him try on several pairs of heels? He needs to learn the proper way of walking in them."

"I will be glad to help you with this, it will be fun seeing my macho brother, tottering in women's shoes, but what are you going to do while we are out humiliating your husband?

"I will tell you the whole story another time, suffice it to say, I have some preparations of my own to make."

Harold's face flushed with embarrassment at the thought of trying on women's clothing and walking in heels. But he knew he couldn't refuse his sister's request. With a reluctant nod, he followed her out of the house and into a world that was completely foreign to him.

Reluctantly, Harold climbed into the backseat of Monica's car, feeling exposed and vulnerable. He couldn't help but wonder what people would think if they saw him with his sister, a crossdresser, and his apparent driver. But deep down, he understood her reasoning - no woman would want to be seen with someone like him. The word 'fag' echoed in his mind, a term he had never associated with himself before. But after his encounter with Master Alexander and the memory of Susan taking the monster cock without flinching, he couldn't help but question his desires.

As they made their way to the entrance, Harold could feel the disapproving stares and hear the snide comments from other shoppers.

He couldn't help but wonder what his sister was telling people about him.

She trailed behind him, clearly trying to distance herself as much as possible. When she caught sight of a passing man, she smiled and pointed Harold out to him, most likely making some cruel remark about her cross-dressing brother.

Finally, Monica reached him and impatiently asked why he was lagging behind. "I don't know where I'm supposed to go," he admitted.

"Ugh, just follow me. But stay far enough away so no one thinks we're together," she instructed.

Monica took her time leading him through the crowded mall, purposely making him pass by as many people as possible. Harold wanted to hurry up and get this over with, but he knew better than to speak up.

Finally, they arrived at the lingerie store and Monica waved him forward. As he approached her, she stopped and scolded him for not knowing what to buy. "What have you been sneaking from your wife's drawer?" she demanded.

Harold tried to explain that it was all a misunderstanding, but his sister called him a liar and proceeded to give him advice on what he needed to buy - at least six pairs of panties in various colors (though she suggested sticking to red, black, and white), a garter belt (preferably black with a red rose), and several pairs of nylons.

Feeling incredibly self-conscious, Harold made his way towards the lingerie section. The thought of buying women's undergarments for himself filled him with shame and embarrassment. He took deep breaths as he started browsing through the racks, hoping not to draw too much attention from other shoppers.

Just then, a sales clerk approached him with a friendly smile. "Can I help you find something, sir?" she asked, sensing his confusion and discomfort. "Are you shopping for your wife or perhaps a girlfriend?"

Harold could sense that the woman probably knew the truth just from the look on his face and the fact that he was wearing a skirt but he also knew that his instructions were to tell anyone who asked that he was shopping for himself.

"They are for me," he said in a voice barely above a whisper.'

"What did you say?" she asked.

Harold raised his voice slightly and repeated that the lingerie was for his personal use.

"You seem a little embarrassed. Surely you have bought lingerie for yourself before?"

Harold didn't know how to answer, if he told her the truth he would be violating Susan's directive not to try and justify his crossdressing by blaming her.

"No ma'am, I have always had someone to buy them for me. This is my first attempt.

Just then Harold saw another man step out of the changing booth wearing nothing but a black bra and black panties. He walked over to a large black woman sitting on a bench and asked her what she thought. She answered that she would have to raise his daily doses of estrogen to increase the size of his breasts but other than that she was pleased with his selections. "Go get 5 more pairs, two in black and three in red. "Yes, Mistress," he replied.

Seeing this Harold felt a little better but hearing her words about giving her man estrogen, made him nervous. He hadn't even thought that she might try to alter the shape of his body by giving him female hormones but she had said that she was going to feminize him so he saw it as something she might do.

Harold and Monica had finally managed to finish their shopping spree. Monica had helped Harold select the proper panties, garter belts, nylons, and brassieres in a variety of colors. She even found a few items on sale that they were able to snap up.

"Now to get you a pair of heels. I can't wait to see you teetering on 6-inch heels", Monica told him.

The idea scared Harold almost to the point of crying, but he was fairly sure that his sister would not find any shoes with that high of heels in the mall.

She had forced Harold to put on the red bra, black garter belt, red panties, and a pair of black nylons so now as he walked with his white blouse, gray skirt, and black sandals everyone could see the nylons with his leg hair pushing through. Harold was humiliated and things were only going to get worse.

When they reached a high-end shoe store, Monica told Harold to go in and begin browsing the women's section until a sales clerk approached him. Then he was to tell her that he wanted a pair of the highest heels that they had, in his size.

Harold had wandered around the aisles for a few minutes when a sales clerk approached him. When she reached him and asked him what he was looking for his heart pounded in his chest. Monica had instructed him to ask for the highest heels they had, in his size. The store assistant looked up from her computer, her brow furrowed in confusion.

"Sir, are you sure you want the highest heels we have? It might not be the most comfortable, especially for someone new to wearing heels," she cautioned.

Harold hesitated, the embarrassment of being in a women's shoe store multiplied tenfold. But he knew he had to follow his sister's orders.

"Yes, please. I need a pair that will make me look... more feminine," he stammered, making his way over to the display of heels.

The sales assistant couldn't help but chuckle to herself as she carefully selected a pair of sleek, black stilettos in Harold's size. She handed them to him with a sly smile, shaking her head in disbelief at the sight of this burly man trying on such dainty shoes. "Would you like to try them on, sir?" she asked, unable to contain her amusement.

"Yes, please," Harold responded, determined to prove that he could wear these shoes just like any other woman.

Walking over to a nearby bench, Harold sat down and slipped off his sandals. He couldn't help but feel self-conscious as people glanced at him curiously. He ignored their stares and focused on fitting his foot into the first shoe. His toes were slightly cramped but he hoped that in time the shoes would mold to his feet. With a deep breath, he slipped on the second shoe and tried to stand up, only to have his ankle give out from under him. He cried out in pain and looked up to see Monica standing over him with a look of concern.

"I think you need to practice on something a little lower before you can conquer that pair," she said gently, motioning for the sales clerk to find a pair with a more manageable three-inch heel.

After a few minutes, the sales clerk returned with a pair of black, three-inch heels. Monica nodded in approval and told Harold to try those on instead.

Harold hesitated for a moment, but then he knew that he had to obey his sister. He slipped off his sandals and replaced them with the new shoes. The three-inch heels felt much more comfortable, and he was able to stand up straight without difficulty.

As Harold stood there in his new heels, he couldn't help but feel a strange sense of pride. He had never felt so feminine before, and the feel of the shoes on his feet was exhilarating.

Monica gave him a playful pat on the cheek. "See, Harold? You can do anything I ask you to do. Now let's go find your matching purse and handbag."

Harold shrugged, still feeling a bit embarrassed but also a bit excited at the same time. He followed her to the register where he paid for both pairs of shoes.

"Would you like to wear your new shoes, out of the store, sir?" she asked him.

"Yes, that would be best," Monica broke in. Just put the sandals in the bag."

Harold returned to the bench put on the three-inch heels and followed his sister out of the mall.

Chapter Fifteen-Trapped in Pleasure: Susan's Bondage Adventure

As Harold and Monica were finishing their shopping spree for his new wardrobe, Susan was occupied with her own tasks. She carefully carried the bags Master Alexander had entrusted to her on her walk home, eagerly anticipating what they contained. As she entered her room, she placed the bags on her bed and eagerly began to open them.

The first item she pulled out was a sleek, black leather harness. Studying it in front of her, she could already imagine how it would hug her body and accentuate her curves. Two large metal rings beckoned to be filled by her breasts, making her heart race with anticipation.

Excited to try it on, Susan resisted the urge to strip off all her clothing and instead decided to inspect the rest of the contents first. The next item that caught her eye was a wide slave collar also made of black leather. She attempted to fasten it around her neck but found that it pushed her head up too high, making it clear that assistance would be needed.

Amidst the pile of items in the bag, she discovered an array of small padlocks, one of which she assumed was meant to secure the collar around her neck. A surge of excitement coursed through her veins at the thought of being adorned with these symbols of submission.

Just as she was admiring the items and wondering what Master Alexander had planned for her, her phone rang. She eagerly answered, overjoyed to hear his voice on the other end.

"Hello," Susan greeted him. "I was just examining the wonderful things you gave me."

"I'm glad you like them. Which is your favorite so far?" Master Alexander asked.

"I am particularly fond of the harness. I can't wait to see what you have in store for me when I wear it. I did try to put on the collar, but

I think I may need some help with that," Susan admitted coyly, already imagining the sensations that would come with wearing it.

Master Alexander chuckled warmly at Susan's confession, his voice growing deeper and more commanding. "Ah, my dear, you are right. The harness will fit you perfectly, and that collar, once secured, will be the ultimate symbol of your devotion. It seems we have a task at hand that requires two people. I would have you come to me, now but you have other things that you need to accomplish before we meet again. Do you remember telling me about the Minister who stopped and offered you a ride?"

"Yes, of course, he is the minister at the Methodist Church that Harold and I attend. Why?"

I imagine that he will be giving a sermon designed to shame you in front of the congregation. You will be in the front pew while he delivers that sermon. Now, here is what you will do?"

Susan's heart raced with anticipation and apprehension. She knew that this was a significant step for her, one that would change her life forever. But that thrill of uncertainty only heightened her desire to please her Master, to be his obedient slave.

The following Sunday morning, Susan put on her shortest black leather skirt, a bright red blouse, and her high boots. The entire congregation watched her as she walked down the center aisle towards the front pew.

Susan smiled as she saw several men staring at her with obvious lust in their eyes. A couple of women looked like they might have a stroke as they watched her proceed.

Susan arrived at the very front row and sat down, at first he legs tightly together, but then she realized what Master Alexander wanted from her. So spreading her legs slightly she knew that the minister would be able to see her unshaven pussy as he looked down at her.

Susan smiled as several men hurried trying to get seats close to her only to have their wives or girlfriends grab them by the ears and force them into their pews. Finally, the service started, first with the singing of hymns and then the sermon itself.

The Title of today's sermon is The Beauty of Modesty: A Sermon on Humility and Grace" The minister began.

Heavenly Father,

As we gather here today, we ask for Your guidance and wisdom to illuminate our hearts and minds as we explore the concept of modesty.

Help us to understand its significance in our lives and how it reflects Your divine nature. May Your Spirit be present among us, leading us into deeper understanding and transformation. In Your holy name, Amen.

Dear brothers and sisters in Christ,

Today, I want us to reflect on the timeless virtue of modesty. In a world that often celebrates self-promotion and excess, modesty stands as a beacon of humility and grace. It is a virtue deeply rooted in the teachings of Christ and serves as a powerful reminder of our call to live lives of purpose, dignity, and reverence.

Let us turn to the Scriptures for guidance on the virtue of modesty. In 1 Timothy 2:9-10, the apostle Paul writes, "I also want the women to dress modestly, with decency and propriety, adorning themselves, not with elaborate hairstyles or gold or pearls or expensive clothes, but with good deeds, appropriate for women who profess to worship God."

Here, Paul emphasizes that true beauty is found not in outward adornment, but in the adornment of good deeds and a heart devoted to God. Similarly, in 1 Peter 3:3-4, we read, "Your beauty should not come from outward adornments, such as elaborate hairstyles and the wearing of gold jewelry or fine clothes. Rather, it should be that of your inner self, the unfading beauty of a gentle and quiet spirit, which is of great worth in God's sight."

These passages remind us that our worth and beauty are not determined by external appearances or material possessions but by the condition of our hearts and the character we cultivate.

Understanding Modesty:

What then, does it mean to live a life of modesty? Modesty encompasses not only how we dress but also how we carry ourselves, how we speak, and how we interact with others. At its core, modesty is about humility, self-respect, and reverence for God.

In our modern context, the concept of modesty is often associated with clothing choices, particularly for women. While dressing modestly is important, true modesty goes beyond mere outward appearances. It is about cultivating a spirit of humility and dignity in all aspects of our lives.

Living Modestly:

So, how can we embody modesty in our daily lives? Let us consider a few practical steps:

Cultivate Humility: Modesty begins with humility, recognizing that we are not defined by our possessions or achievements but by our relationship with God. Let us humble ourselves before Him, acknowledging our dependence on His grace.

Guard Your Heart: Modesty involves guarding our hearts against pride, envy, and selfishness. Let us fill our minds with thoughts that are pure, noble, and uplifting, seeking to align our desires with God's will.

Practice Gratitude: A modest heart is a grateful heart. Let us cultivate an attitude of gratitude, recognizing and appreciating the blessings God has bestowed upon us, both big and small.

Serve Others: True modesty is expressed through acts of service and kindness towards others. Let us look for opportunities to serve those in need, showing love and compassion as Christ did.

Conclusion:

Dear friends, as we reflect on the virtue of modesty, may we be inspired to live lives that honor God and reflect His grace and love. Let us adorn ourselves not with the trappings of this world but with the virtues of humility, dignity, and compassion.

As we go forth from this place, may we shine as beacons of light in a world that desperately needs the message of Christ's love. May our lives bear witness to the beauty of modesty, drawing others closer to the heart of God.

Closing Prayer:

Heavenly Father,

We thank You for the gift of Your Word and the wisdom it imparts to our hearts. Help us, Lord, to embody the virtue of modesty in all that we do, reflecting Your grace and love to the world around us. May our lives be a testimony to Your goodness and faithfulness.

In Jesus' name, Amen.

The minister's voice quivered as he tried to finish the sermon, sweat pouring down his face and drenching his collar. His eyes were drawn helplessly to Susan's open legs, exposed by her scandalously short skirt. Trying to block out the sinful thoughts filling his mind, he forced himself to complete the service. But he couldn't resist stealing glances at Susan, imagining all the things he wanted to do between her spread thighs. Fighting against his desires, the minister struggled to maintain composure and resisted giving in to temptation. Finally, with a tremble in his hands, he turned away from the congregation and rushed to the vestry, unable to face them with his arousal throbbing painfully in his pants.

Susan rose and began to walk toward the exit imagining the tongue thrashing she would get from the members of the congregation. Of course, the only person that had seen her cunt was the Minister but surely some of the others had recognized what she was doing.

So she was surprised when the minister's wife, approached her before she could leave. "Susan, that was quite an exhibition you put on for my dear husband. I need to thank you for that since I am sure that I will receive the benefit of his lust tonight. Maybe I can even get him to do something more than the missionary position, so thank you. And by the way, I love those boots, where can I get a pair?"

"I order them online, you can't get a decent heel at the mall."

"Well, you will have to give me the URL. And thank you again for getting my husband's juices flowing."

Chapter Sixteen-That Night at the Williams' House.

As the last clinking of silverware faded away and Mary Williams cleared the dinner dishes, she turned to her husband, Purvis. Her voice was tight with tension as she spoke. "What did you think of the way Susan was dressed today, dear?"

Purvis shifted uncomfortably in his chair, afraid to answer. The look on his wife's face told him that she had been watching him more closely than listening to his sermon.

"It was inappropriate and disgusting," he finally answered, trying to sound stern and authoritative. "I need to gather the elders and go to her home to admonish her never to wear anything like that again."

Mary's eyes narrowed in anger as she slammed down a plate. "You will do no such thing," she declared, her voice rising in volume. "Drop your piousness for a moment and tell the truth. You may have thought you got away with sneaking into the back room, but I saw it before you could turn completely around. The tent in your pants was all too clear. What were you thinking of doing to Susan as you stared at her exposed body?"

The air crackled with tension as Mary's accusation hung between them like a heavy fog. Purvis could feel his cheeks burning with shame and guilt as he struggled to come up with an excuse. But in his heart, he knew that Mary was right - he had let temptation cloud his thoughts and betray his vows.

"You still haven't answered my questions, Purvis. What were you thinking about when you were looking at the cunt of one of your congregation?"

"Mary please let this go. I am ashamed enough, without having to elocute to you my lust."

Mary walked out of the room and when she came back she was wearing a long black negligee and black slippers with a kitten heel.

The air crackled with tension, thick like a heavy fog that surrounded them. Mary's accusation hung in the air, sharp and accusatory. Purvis could feel his cheeks burning with shame and guilt as he struggled to come up with an excuse, his mind racing with guilt and regret.

But deep down, he knew that Mary was right - he had let temptation cloud his thoughts and betray his vows. He could feel the weight of his mistakes bearing down on him, suffocating him.

"I know this isn't what you were fantasizing about, but let's go to bed," Mary spoke with a hint of sadness in her voice. "I will try my best to satisfy you. I won't mind if you close your eyes and pretend it's Susan's cunt that you're putting your cock inside of."

Purvis felt a flash of surprise at Mary's words - she had never spoken so boldly before. Her language shocked him, making him realize just how much he didn't know about his wife.

"What has gotten into you, Mary?" he asked incredulously. "I have never heard you use such language."

"Does it shock you, dear? Are you flabbergasted that your prim and proper wife is just a slut in disguise?" Mary retorted, her tone daring him to judge her.

Unexpectedly, Purvis reached down and scooped Mary up into his arms. Despite his out-of-shape body, he hurried as fast as he could towards their bedroom. Dropping her onto the bed in the middle of their room, Purvis quickly stripped off his clothes.

As his shorts hit the floor with a soft thud, Mary's gaze was drawn to his now-hard cock - harder than it had been in years. She couldn't help but smile as she thanked Susan for this unexpected gift.

With a breathless moan, she opened her robe and laid back on the bed, spreading her legs wide. The dampness between her legs grew with anticipation and excitement as she waited for her husband to join her.

With a fierce determination, Mary throws off her robe and lies on her back, spreading her legs wide open. Her glistening pussy lips invite Purvis in, wet with her juices and pulsing with desire. Despite her age, Mary's body is still toned and beautiful, driving Purvis mad with lust.

He stares hungrily at his wife's black pussy hair, wishing it were blonde but unable to resist the urge to climb between her thighs. His rough fingers spread the lips of her vulva, plunging first one and then two digits inside as he prepares her for their passionate union.

Mary moans loudly as she feels herself being prepared for pleasure by her husband's skilled hands. She fantasizes about inviting Susan to join them, knowing that if anyone could rev Purvis' engine like this, it would be her.

Finally, Purvis positions himself at the entrance to her dripping sex and slides his throbbing cock up and down her slick slit, teasing her sensitive nub until she cries out in ecstasy.

With her legs splayed open and her hips arching, Mary's eyes locked onto his erect cock, taunting her with its promise of pleasure. Her body screamed for relief, the sweaty skin of her inner thighs sticking together as she writhed beneath him. It was time.

Purvis held his breath, his eyes locked onto his wife's exposed flesh. He pushed inside her, the resistance of her tight pussy gripping him like a vice. Both of them sucked in a sharp breath as he sank into her.

Mary gasped, her eyes fluttering shut as she felt him invade her. She wrapped her legs around his waist, pulling him deeper into her. Her nails dug into his back, the pain a welcome sensation against the overwhelming pleasure coursing through her veins.

Their bodies moved in time, the wet slapping of skin echoing through the room. Mary's breaths came in rapid gasps as Purvis' hips thrashed against hers. Her pussy clenched around his cock, her body convulsing in waves of pleasure.

Mary let out a loud moan, her orgasm a tidal wave crashing over her. She clawed at Purvis' back, her nails drawing blood as she rode out the waves of pleasure.

Purvis' climax built, a tightness growing in his groin. He thrust harder, his cock sliding in and out of his wife's wet pussy.

With a final cry, Purvis erupted inside her, his cock twitching as he filled her with his seed. Mary moaned, her nails raking down his back as more waves of pleasure washed over her. With her legs splayed open and her hips arching, Mary's eyes locked onto his erect cock, taunting her with its promise of pleasure. Her body screamed for relief, the sweaty skin of her inner thighs sticking together as she writhed beneath him. It was time.

Purvis held his breath, his eyes locked onto his wife's exposed flesh. He pushed inside her, the resistance of her tight pussy gripping him like a vice. Both of them sucked in a sharp breath as he sank into her.

Mary gasped, her eyes fluttering shut as she felt him invade her. She wrapped her legs around his waist, pulling him deeper into her. Her nails dug into his back, the pain a welcome sensation against the overwhelming pleasure coursing through her veins.

Their bodies moved in time, the wet slapping of skin echoing through the room. Mary's breaths came in rapid gasps as Purvis' hips thrashed against hers. Her pussy clenched around his cock, her body convulsing in waves of pleasure.

Mary let out a loud moan, her orgasm a tidal wave crashing over her. She clawed at Purvis' back, her nails drawing blood as she rode out the waves of pleasure.

From that day forward, their lovemaking was infused with a newfound passion and desire. They would spend hours exploring each other's bodies, discovering new ways to please one another. The thought of Susan was never far from their minds, but in the end, it was the connection between Purvis and Mary that truly mattered.

As the years went by, the church elders never confronted Susan about her clothing choices. In fact, she would often wear even shorter skirts on Sundays, her eyes hinting at a secret she shared with Purvis and Mary. The once-strict minister and his wife had found a side of themselves they never knew existed, all thanks to one woman's daring fashion choice.

Mary became close friends with Susan many times revealing how much she appreciated Susan and telling her all the new things that Purvis was doing to satisfy her. Susan would then pass that information to Master Alexander. He always seemed pleased hearing that the Minister was becoming addicted to sex although he wished that Susan could find a way to seduce the man. Only when that was accomplished would he feel he had accomplished his mission.

Susan smiled to herself as she relayed Mary's latest confessions to Master Alexander. She could sense his growing satisfaction and anticipation, but she knew that he would not be truly content until she had seduced the minister. Susan had always relished the challenge, and she was determined to succeed.

As the weeks passed, Susan continued to push the boundaries of acceptable attire, her skirts growing shorter and more daring. The church elders turned a blind eye, but the minister couldn't help but take notice. His eyes lingered on her legs, and he found himself growing increasingly distracted during his sermons.

One Sunday, as Susan walked up the aisle towards her seat, she felt the minister's gaze upon her. She turned to meet his eyes, her lips curling into a knowing smile. She could see the desire simmering beneath the surface, and she knew that the moment was ripe. Brazenly she walked over to the Minister. He looked down blushing with embarrassment but Susan put her hand under his chin and lifted his head forcing him to look into her eyes.

"Do I excite you, Purvis? What would you like to do with me?"

"I can't talk about this here." He stammered.

"Tell me where and when and I will be there," Susan said.

"After the service in the vestry. Do you know how to get there?"

"Not without the congregation seeing me. Wouldn't you feel more comfortable coming to my house? Harold wouldn't mind. And bring Mary with you, I am sure she will enjoy it. Shall we say about 7?"

Chapter Seventeen-Seducing the Masses

The preacher's sermon was a little hard to follow that day as his mind seemed to wander at the wrong times. Finally, it came to a conclusion and as Susan was walking out she encountered Mary.

"Oh hello dear, I particularly like your outfit today. I always think that leather is so exciting. You might want to wear a shorter version in the future, however," Mary told her.

"I am glad that I was able to catch you before I left today," Susan
began. "I invited Harold to come over to the house tonight and I want
you to accompany him. I hope that you won't mind if I seduce him as
long as I provide some much younger male company for you?"

"Oh my, I hadn't thought of having sex with any other man," Mary replied.

"You will when you see the one that I will have for you tonight. Will you come?"

"I can't wait. I am getting a little wet between my folds just thinking about it."

As Susan climbed into her car she took out her cell phone and called Master Alexander. "Master," she began when he answered. "The time has finally arrived. The Minister and his wife will be at my house tonight at 7. Would you like to join us? I promised Mary that while I was fucking her husband that a much younger man would be fucking her. I hope that isn't a problem."

"No, that is perfect. We can get two birds at once. Do you think that you can get him to do all the things that we have discussed?"

"With a little help from you, I think your plan will come off flawlessly."

At precisely 7 o'clock that evening, the doorbell rang and Susan instructed Harold, dressed in all his feminine glory to answer the door.

Reverend Williams and his wife, Mary, couldn't help but let out a
small laugh when they saw Harold standing before them in the attire of
a French Maid. His face flushed with embarrassment as he realized the
couple knew his true identity and were teasing him.

"Did you know that Susan had a maid?" Purvis asked his wife.

"I had heard something about that," Mary replied with a sly grin.
"Doesn't she look absolutely stunning?"

Harold's cheeks burned even brighter with embarrassment as he silently followed the couple into the house. As they entered the living room, they were met with quite a sight. Susan stood before them in nothing but red lingerie, while Master Alexander greeted them completely naked.

Both Mary and Purvis gasped in shock at the size of Master Alexander's massive phallus, hanging heavily between his legs.

"Oh my," Mary exclaimed, her eyes widening in awe. "Is this Greek God for me? I do believe that if he puts that majestic piece of cock meat inside of me, he will split me wide open."

Susan chuckled at her friend's reaction. "No, dear," she interjected. "He won't split you, but he will stretch you like no other man has ever done before. You've heard the old saying, haven't you? A cunt will stretch a mile before it tears an inch."

Mary's eyes widened as she took in the sight before her. She couldn't help but feel a strange mix of both fear and excitement.

"Are you sure about this, Susan?" she asked, her voice trembling slightly. She glanced at Purvis, seeking reassurance from her husband.

Purvis stepped forward and took Mary's hand, giving it a comforting squeeze. "It's up to you, love," he said quietly. "But I trust Susan and Master Alexander. They know what they're doing."

Inwardly, Purvis was a mix of apprehension and arousal. He'd never seen his wife so turned on, and he couldn't deny the sense of adventure that was coursing through him. But he also knew that he couldn't let his wife do anything she wasn't completely comfortable with but he also knew that for him to get what he wanted, Mary would want some degree of reciprocation.

"Why don't you two get out of your clothes?" Susan asked as she slipped the bra from her magnificent breasts and pulled the panties off revealing a cunt with heart-shaped blonde pussy hair. "Harriet, you should also get rid of the dress and your panties just in case there is a need for your man cunt."

"Yes, Mistress," Harold replied although he had not anticipated being a part of the orgy. He thought that he was just here to witness and to serve.

Susan took Purvis's hand and led him to the large leather sofa. She lay down on her back, spread her legs wide, and reached for his now hard cock. "You have a nice cock, Purvis," she begins. "You don't know how long I have wanted to see you naked." She stretched the skin of his uncut cock back as far as it would go and then slowly pushed it back over the head of his cock drawing a small dollop of precum to his piss slit. With her other hand, she wiped that morsel off onto her fingers and then brought them into her mouth. "Mmm that tastes so good," she moaned.

Purvis almost ejaculated right then as he listened to the sexy seductress. "I am ready for you," Susan crooned. With "that, Purvis crawled on top of Susan and lowered himself so that his cock was close to her wet dripping cunt. Susan reached between their bodies and took

Purvis cock in her hand guiding it to her slippery opening. Feeling his cock slip inside her Purvis let his weight down pushing his cock deep inside of the woman that he had been lusting after for almost a year. "Of god, that feels like I am in Heaven," the preacher exclaimed.

"That's it, Purvis, tell me what you think of my cunt."

"I love your cunt, Susan," he replied.

"I don't want to hear about your love, I want you to tell me that you worship me?"

"So deeply drowning in his lust the Minister didn't even realize that he was being led down a path of sin and eventual destruction.

As Susan's words echoed in his ears, Purvis couldn't help but feel an overwhelming sense of desire and submission. He had never felt this way before, but there was something undeniably powerful about Susan's command that made him want to please her in every way possible.

Mary watched from the sidelines, her eyes wide with both surprise and arousal. She had never seen her husband like this, and the prospect of experiencing new and taboo pleasures was both exhilarating and terrifying.

Harold, on the other hand, could only stare in awe. He had been around many lustful encounters, but nothing like this. The sight of the Reverend deep inside Susan, worshipping her cunt, was a sight he would never forget.

As Purvis continued to thrust into Susan, the room grew increasingly heated. The sounds of their bodies mingling filled the air, and the scent of their arousal filled the room. Susan moaned and writhed beneath him, her hands gripping his hips as she urged him on.

Master Alexander watched from the corner, his eyes never leaving the spectacle before him. He knew what would happen next, and it excited him to no end.

In a sudden burst of energy, Purvis let out a primal cry and thrust into Susan one last time. He had never felt anything like this before, and it was as if the world had fallen away, leaving only him and Susan in their passionate embrace.

Susan's lips brushed against Purvis' ear as she whispered seductively, "Oh, Reverend, you're just aching to be my devoted disciple now, aren't you?" Her sultry tone sent shivers down his spine as he nodded in silent agreement, entranced by her commanding presence.

Purvis was rooted to the spot, Susan's breathy whisper still vibrating through his ear. He blinked, his gaze locked into Susan's smoky eyes, feeling an unfamiliar tug of submission pull at his core. Something about her - her presence, allure - had him completely ensnared. He realized then that he was willing to cross any line for her.

Susan beamed back at him, a thrilling surge of power rippling through her veins. Purvis, with his brawny build and puppy-dog eyes, was now hers in every sense of the word. Ownership had never tasted this sweet.

From a shadowy corner, Mary stood wide-eyed at the sight unfolding before her. Her heart pounded against her ribs as she watched her husband, completely bewitched by another woman. The raw sexual energy between Purvis and Susan was palpable.

Harold watched on too, captivated. He'd never seen their master, Alexander, so deeply aroused and equally entranced by the spectacle of Reverend Purvis driven to carnal madness by Susan.

As Purvis wrestled back control from the orgasm that had sent him spiraling to different galaxies, he noted through lust-clouded eyes his wife exiting hand-in-hand with Master Alexander. He forced himself upright off of Susan's warm curves and onto shaky legs.

"Alexander wouldn't...he won't harm her?" Purvis stammered out the question to Susan, worry creasing his features.

"Come on," Susan winked back at him, "Let's keep an eye on them." She sauntered ahead, her pert backside taunting him with each step they took. The sight of her bare ass had him stiffening with desire again. A naughty curiosity started gnawing at him - what would it feel like to take her from behind? The very thought made him throb with renewed vigor.

Harold felt a twinge of unease creep up his spine. Unsure of how to proceed, he figured it best to tail along just in case he was needed. He climbed the stairs behind the duo, his heart pounding in anticipation. Entering the room, he was met with the intoxicating sight of the minister's wife spread out on his bed. His member strained against the confines of his lace panties at the sight, and remembering his wife's previous order, he discarded them into a corner.

Master Alexander ascended between Mary's open, inviting thighs, teasing her sensitive folds with the powerful bulge that strained against his pants. The sultry scent of her arousal filled the air, causing her to whimper in anticipation. Observing the scene from afar, Purvis felt an overpowering urge to intervene, only to be halted by Susan's calming touch on his arm. "You must let this unravel naturally or all will be lost," she whispered delicately yet firmly.

Purvis was confused by her cryptic statement yet found he couldn't deny the allure of Susan's touch, a woman he had only recently shared a night of passion with. It was as though her intoxicating essence drew him in relentlessly. A burning lust consumed him for this enigmatic woman and he realized he would willingly submit to her commands.

Mary's moans echoed through the room as Master Alexander slowly unveiled his imposing manhood, its head nudging at her entrance, stretching her boundaries far more than any lover before him. He paused briefly, allowing her time to adjust to his intimidating size. "Do you wish me to stop, Mary?" he asked in a husky voice, already knowing her answer.

"Jesus... no. Please... give it to me but ease into it. I want to feel you as deep inside me as you can manage but... your size... god... I need some time." She said breathlessly, overcome by the sheer intensity of their connection.

"As you desire, my sweet," Master Alexander responded before easing another couple of inches into her welcoming warmth. Again he paused, allowing her body to adapt to his size.

"That's... breathtaking..." Mary managed between gasps as she adjusted.

Master Alexander continued to tease her, moving slowly in and out of her dripping wet pussy, making her feel completely overwhelmed with pleasure. Mary's walls began to tighten around his thrusts, tugging him deeper into her, pulling him closer and closer to the edge.

As Master Alexander's formidable manhood further invaded Mary's velvety depths, her moans of ecstasy vibrated off the walls. He was thick and hard, like a pulsating beacon of pleasure that filled her completely. She could feel every vein, every ridge of his engorged member inside her, stretching her in the most delicious way possible.

"Feel good?" Master Alexander teased, grinding his hips against hers in slow, deliberate circles. His sable eyes twinkled with mischief as he watched her struggle to regain composure.

"Oh God, yes," she gasped, arching her back to meet his thrusts. "Don't stop." Her words were heavy with raw desire and unadulterated lust.

Meanwhile, Purvis was entranced by Susan's sultry sway as they watched their counterparts. The sight was devilishly decadent - a serpentine dance of carnal desire unfurling ever so tantalizingly before their eyes. He couldn't tear his gaze away from Susan's sumptuous derriere - it beckoned him like a siren calling out to a lost sailor. His cock throbbed painfully in anticipation, longing for the unknown path that lay ahead.

Susan turned around and smiled coyly at Purvis, "Like what you see?" She let out a soft laugh before approaching him. There was no hesitation or embarrassment in her actions; she wanted him and wasn't afraid to show it.

Reaching down, Susan gingerly wrapped her slender fingers around Purvis' throbbing erection – eliciting a sharp intake of breath from the preacher. Her touch was feather-light yet firm, causing waves of unadulterated pleasure to ripple through his body.

Purvis found himself drawn into the magnetic pull of Susan's cerulean eyes. His heart pounded in his chest as if it were trying to escape its cage. Wordlessly, he nodded his consent, surrendering himself to her devilish charm.

A symphony of moans and gasps filled the room as Master Alexander quickened his pace. His thick cock pistoned in and out of Mary - their bodies slick with sweat. He gripped her thighs tightly, pulling her closer, burying himself deeper.

"Can you take more?" he asked, a wicked grin plastered on his face. Mary responded by wrapping her legs tightly around him and pleading for more.

"Please...more," she cried out, her voice laced with eagerness and urgency.

With renewed vigor, Master Alexander began rhythmically pumping into Mary unchecked. Every powerful thrust rocked her to her core; each retreat left her yearning for more. The room was filled with the lascivious symphony of slapping flesh against flesh - a testament to their unabashed carnality.

Harold hesitantly obeyed his wife's command, his heart pounding in his chest as he bent over and spread his legs. He couldn't believe what was about to happen, but he was powerless to resist Susan's twisted desires.

"That's a good little boy," Susan cooed, running her hand over Harold's exposed ass. "You're going to take every inch of Purvis's cock, aren't you?"

Harold whimpered in response, his mind racing with fear and humiliation. He had never felt so vulnerable, so completely at the mercy of another person.

Purvis approached the foot of the bed, his eyes fixed on Harold's exposed hole. "I can't believe I'm actually going to do this," he muttered, his hands shaking with nervousness.

"Believe it, Reverend," Susan said, a cruel smile twisting her lips. "You're going to be my bitch from now on."

With that, Purvis pressed the head of his cock against Harold's entrance, slowly pushing inside. Harold cried out in pain as Purvis filled him up, his cock stretching him to the limit.

"Oh God, it hurts," Harold sobbed, tears streaming down his face.

"Shut up and take it like a man," Susan snapped, slapping Harold across the ass. "You're my property now, and you'll do as I say."

Purvis began to thrust in and out of Harold, each stroke driving him deeper inside. Harold could feel himself being torn apart, his insides on fire with pain. But at the same time, there was a strange sense of pleasure, a perverse thrill at being used in such a degrading way.

Susan watched with sadistic delight as her husband and the reverend became one, their bodies joined in a twisted union of pain and pleasure. She knew that this was just the beginning of their torment, and she couldn't wait to see what other sick games she could come up with.

When the minister finally ejaculated inside of Harold he pulled out his cock dripping with his cum and other bodily fluids.

As the erotic scene unfolded around them, Mary found herself on her knees before Master Alexander, reverently worshipping his still throbbing member with fervent kisses and licks. She savored the combined taste of their shared climax, each salty drop teasing her tongue like a decadent dessert she couldn't get enough of.

Master Alexander watched as she eagerly drank from him, proving her commitment to serve and please him as he pleased. A sense of primal satisfaction washed over him as Mary's pledge echoed in his ears.

"Yes Master," Mary breathed against his semi-hard cock, sending shivers up his spine. "I will bring others to you... I will willingly teach them your ways..."

The room crackled with sexual tension and unspoken desires; an enticing promise of more nights filled with pleasure and raw passion yet to come.

Chapter Eighteen-A New Religion.

By the time that the night was over, both Mary and Purvis had agreed to become the servants of Master Alexander and Susan.

"I have a special task for you preacher," Alexander said to Purvis. "You are going to bring your entire congregation to me."

"How am I supposed to do that?" Purvis asked him.

"By delivering the sermons that I write. Just as you have used your words to praise your God, you will now use them to praise me."

Purvis looked at him and saw that an aura had surrounded him

For the first time, Purvis realized who he was dealing with. "I can't do that it would cost me my soul," he complained.

"You have already forfeited your soul. If you obey me, you will live a long and very exciting life enjoying an endless supply of your beautiful women and young willing men, if not you will never again know the bliss of sex with a woman or man, and when you die you will come to me and feel my wrath.

While Purvis was considering what Master Alexander had suggested, his wife was making up her own mind.

She approached Master Alexander, her body trembling with a mix of fear and reverence. She dropped to her knees, bowing her head until her forehead touched his feet.

"Tell me, Master. What is your will?" she whispered, her voice filled with devotion and submission.

"Rise, my slave. There is much for you to do," Master Alexander commanded, his deep voice sending chills down Susan's spine.

Susan turned to Mary, shocked to see that 30 years had melted away from her face and body. In their place stood a gorgeous raven-haired beauty, radiating youth and vitality. Without a word, Susan rushed to her vanity and grabbed a small handheld mirror. Holding it in front of Mary's face, she watched as the reflection transformed into an image of herself.

"What...what is happening to me?" Mary whispered in disbelief, her eyes wide with confusion and fear.

"This, my dear, is the true blessing of surrendering to us," Susan replied, her voice dripping with excitement. "Your soul is now bound to us and as a result, you will remain forever youthful and beautiful."

Mary looked at the mirror again, feeling a newfound power and confidence coursing through her veins. She knew that she would do anything to maintain this state.

With renewed purpose and devotion, Susan whispered instructions to Mary on their plan to bring their unsuspecting victims to their knees.

The following Sunday, Pastor Williams stood before the congregation. After an opening prayer that didn't end with the traditional "in Jesus' name," he began his sermon.

"My dear friends. I have had an epiphany," he announced in a tone that demanded attention. "Just as God came to Moses on Mount Horeb and the angel appeared to our beloved Virgin Mary, He came to me in a dream last night." The congregation murmured in shock at this statement.

"He even provided a sign for those who may doubt. Mary, would you please come up?" Pastor Williams beckoned to Mary, whose face now glowed with an otherworldly beauty. The congregation watched in awe as she made her way to the front, ready to fulfill her new purpose in life.

A gasp went up from the gallery as the woman they knew as Mary came to the podium, but not the 60-year-old woman that they were familiar with. This Mary was young and vibrant.

"This is some type of a trick, " a woman declared standing up.

"Please come forward and see for yourself, Gloria," Mary said in a kindly voice.

As Gloria reached the podium she stared openly at Mary. She could see that her best friend was truly transformed from an aged woman to a young beauty.

"My God, how is this possible? I just saw you yesterday and you were as old as I am now. And where is this glow coming from?"

"God restored my youth as a sign that you should believe Purvis when he tells you that he is relaying the word of the Almighty this morning."

Some people had been leaving the church until they heard this exchange. As they settled back in their seats, the preacher continued.

"God told me that I had been misleading his flock although not intentionally. He said that I had also been misled by thousands of years of mistruth. He showed me a vision of our world as it is now, the people depressed, angry, and hopeless. He showed me wars between brothers and political upheaval where there is no clear direction. In the next vision was a world where everyone was smiling, where men of all races lived together in peace and tranquility. There were no political parties because everyone knew what their place was in society.

There was no hunger or poverty, no wars or violence.

Some of the congregation started whispering among themselves, unsure of what to make of all this.

Purvis then stood up from his seat, looking nervous but determined.

"I know that this may sound like blasphemy, but I have been speaking with God. And he has told me that the way to bring about this utopian vision is through submission giving control to a higher authority, and through embracing our base and primal desires."

Susan sat next to him, her eyes shining with devotion and excitement.

"My dear friends, let us not resist this calling. Instead, let us surrender to our divine destiny and allow ourselves to be transformed into the beings that we were always meant to be," she added, her voice full of conviction.

As the sermon continued, the congregation was captivated.

"What do you mean by embracing our base and primal desires?" a woman in the back stood and asked.

"To understand that we must think back to the very beginning when God created Adam and Eve. He didn't give them clothing, as he wanted them to be fully aware of their naked bodies and their natural impulses. They were perfect, bare, and without shame. It wasn't until they ate the forbidden fruit that they became ashamed of their bodies and sought to hide their nakedness.

"That's why we're here today. To return to that state of innocence and purity where all our desires can be freely expressed without fear of retribution or judgment. Where we can all live together in harmony, united in our love for each other and our Creator.

"And this," he said, his voice rising, "this is how we will be saved. By loving each other, by serving each other, and by giving ourselves in surrender to our deepest, most primal desires.

"Listen closely, for I have a proposition that will change your lives forever. No longer will you be bound by societal norms or religious restraints. You are all invited to embrace a new world of unadulterated pleasure and freedom. Let go of your inhibitions, let your sexuality run wild, and offer your bodies willingly to those who desire it."

The church fell into an uneasy silence as Purvis' words hung in the air like a thick fog. Questions and doubts swirled through the congregation.

"What about adultery?" someone called out.

"What about pedophilia?" another shouted.

Purvis' eyes gleamed with fervor as he addressed the questions. "My friends, do not be constrained by archaic beliefs placed upon us by some higher power. God did not create us to be confined to one partner or to reject our natural desires. He did not dictate the rules of marriage or condemn those who love their own family. It is time to break free from these chains and embrace our true selves." The whispers grew louder as some began to question their faith while others were drawn in by Purvis' persuasive words.

"Let us talk about what you call incest. Back in the Garden of Eden God came to the couple and said, "

"And God blessed them, and God said unto them, Be fruitful, and multiply, and replenish the earth, and subdue it: and have dominion over the fish of the sea, and over the fowl of the air, and over every living thing that moveth upon the earth."

The words of the commandment echoed in the very beginning of Genesis, ringing out over the assembled crowd. The speaker, a wise and learned man, explained that it was clear God did not intend for just two individuals to fill the earth by refraining from having sex with only each other. And how could he have expected otherwise, when He had made sex so irresistibly pleasurable? Adam and Eve themselves had children - surely this was a sign that God meant for procreation to occur between more than just one man and one woman. If He had truly wanted to prevent incestuous relationships, then the only individuals allowed to engage in sexual activity would have been the original couple - Adam and Eve. But surely no one believed that was His ultimate purpose?

At the mention of such an absurd idea, an older man near the front spoke up. "But does that still hold today?" he questioned. "I must admit, I too have felt a strong attraction towards my mother. Was it wrong of me to repress those feelings?"

The speaker paused before answering, his expression turning serious. "It wasn't wrong for you," he replied firmly. "You were simply conditioned by societal norms to believe that such sexual pleasure was taboo." The man nodded thoughtfully at this insight, grateful for the clarification.

"Are you saying that there are no restrictions on who we can or cannot engage in sexual activity with?"

"Not from God but you also must know that laws have been passed making some sexual activities illegal and punishable by incarceration.

And while you may want to ignore those laws, remember God's admonition to render unto Caesar the things that are Caesars and to God those things that Gods.

"Then, my dear friends, I urge you all to consider what it means to have faith in God's plan for us and to serve one another with our bodies and souls. It is time to open our hearts and our minds to new possibilities, to love without limits, and to embrace the divine spark within each of us.

"And so, my brothers and sisters, I offer you a choice. You may continue to live in a world of fear, judgment, and scarcity, or you may choose to enter a new era of abundance, harmony, and unconditional love. The choice is yours, but I ask you to consider the consequences of your decision. For if we do not change, we risk plunging ourselves into darkness and despair.

"But if we choose to embrace this new path, we have the opportunity to create a world beyond our wildest dreams. A world where all are equal and free to express themselves without fear or judgment. A world where our bodies and souls are united in love and service to one another and to our Creator. The choice is yours, but remember, the heart that chooses love is the heart that chooses the path to salvation."

With those final words, the congregation remained in stunned silence. No one moved. No one spoke. It was as if the air had been sucked out of the room. And then, slowly, one by one, heads began to bow, hands began to fold over hearts, and tears began to fall.

Purvis stood motionless, his gaze sweeping over the sea of faces before him. He could see the pain and confusion etched across their features, but he also saw hope and a flicker of understanding. And for the first time in a very long time, he felt a sense of purpose and peace.

Mary took his place at the podium. "Dear Sisters, you are all invited to a special meeting this evening. While I would like all females to attend because of secular law I must ask that nobody under the age of 18 attend. We will begin promptly at 7 P.M.

Chapter Nineteen-Mary Introduces Master Alexander to the Congregation

As the appointed hour drew near, women began to arrive at the church. They came in all shapes and sizes, clad in a variety of garments. Some boldly sported short skirts, emulating Susan's style, while others opted for more modest attire. Susan and Mary greeted each woman with a warm smile and urged them to take seats closer to the center aisle, encouraging them to sit as close to the front as possible.

Looking out over the congregation, Mary couldn't help but notice that almost all of the women had made it on time. She felt a sense of pride wash over her - this was going to be a special day. "We'll wait just a few minutes longer," she announced to the group. "Just in case there are any stragglers." With a friendly nod, she added, "Please feel free to chat among yourselves while we wait." The buzz of excitement grew louder as the women exchanged greetings and small talk, eagerly anticipating what was to come.

Finally, Mary stepped to the podium and urged the congregation to come to order. "Dear Friends, I am happy to see that so many of you could attend tonight. I have a special treat for you so without further ado, I will introduce a special guest.

A deafening silence fell over the room as a majestic angel materialized before the women, his bare torso glistening in the soft light. His chiseled muscles rippled like marble beneath perfect skin, drawing every eye in awe and desire.

Their gasps turned to shrieks of terror as the angel slowly undid the button on his leather pants, revealing a massive erection that throbbed with otherworldly power. He stood boldly and unashamed, wings spread wide as if daring anyone to challenge his godlike form.

'Do not be afraid, for I am an angel sent from God to witness to you his new commandments."

"But why are you naked in front of us?" A woman called out.

"This is how God wishes that his people should appear in front of each other. Should I cover up my body and deny you from seeing my magnificence?" he asked them.

The women in the pews exchanged looks with each other, hesitant and uncertain. Some still huddled in prayer, while others whispered to their neighbors.

Susan stepped forward, her eyes fixed on the angel before her. With a deep breath, she spoke, "It is true. Our bodies are sacred, and we should be free to accept and adore each other's beauty without fear or judgment. This is a difficult path, but we must trust in God's plan."

Looking at the congregation, she continued, "Fear not and open your hearts and minds to this new way of being. Unite as one in love and devotion, and together we shall create a world where all may express themselves freely and harmoniously. Embrace the divine spark within each of you and let it guide you through this journey."

The angel watched them, his eyes shining with approval. "So it shall be," he declared

"But we would be ashamed to reveal our bodies to the congregation. Many of us are old and infirm. Others are overweight and wrinkled."

"All of that is your perception. Come forward sister and stand before the congregation."

Nora stepped forward as she had earlier when called up by Mary.

With a swift gesture, Master Alexander's hand crackled with electric energy as he reached out and touched Nora's gray hair. A collective gasp echoed through the room as the gray instantly vanished, replaced by a luscious mane of raven-black hair that shimmered in the light. Nora couldn't believe her eyes as she ran her fingers through her new locks, tears of joy streaming down her face.

But Master Alexander wasn't done yet. "Remove your dress, sister," he commanded, his voice booming with authority.

Trembling with anticipation, Nora unzipped the back of her dress and let it fall to the ground. As she stood in front of everyone, only clad in a plain white bra and cotton panties, she couldn't help but feel self-conscious about her overweight body. And when she reluctantly removed her undergarments at Master Alexander's request, she exposed all of her flaws for everyone to see - sagging breasts, stretch marks, and extra pounds.

But Master Alexander didn't seem phased by any of it. In fact, he seemed excited as he gazed upon Nora's naked form. "Now," he said with a sly smile, "let me transform your body."

Reaching down he touched the gray pubic hair and it turned black as the hair on her head. Nora looked with disbelief seeing her beautiful pubic hair.

Next, Alexander touched her breast. The congregation watched in wonderment as her skin began to contract, her once-sagging breasts were firm and beautiful.

"Now, you who have gathered here today, behold the truth that I have brought to you. Your bodies, as they are, are the vessels of your divine essence. They are the temples of God. And it is through the sacred act of love, of uniting yourselves, in sacred communion with each other, that you shall bring forth new life, that you shall create a world of harmony and unity.

"And do not be afraid," he continued, "for in this world, there is no right or wrong, no good or evil. Only love and light. And it is through this love that you shall find your true purpose, your divine calling. Sisters continue to witness God's power to restore you to the perfect form that he intended for you.

He touched Nora again and she was transformed into a woman of 25 years. Not an ounce of excess fat could be detected anywhere on her body. Her legs were perfectly formed from the bottoms of her feet to the v where they connected to her torso. The rest of her body was perfectly toned.

As the angel continued to speak, he made his way around the room, laying his hands upon the women one by one. With each touch, they too were transformed; their skin glowed with an otherworldly radiance, their bodies became more svelt, and their hair turned to the most luxurious locks they had ever seen.

The room was filled with gasps and cries of delight as each woman received her divine makeover. Some had dreamed of having perfect bodies since they were young girls, while others had accepted their flaws as an unchangeable part of themselves. Now they were being gifted with the bodies they had always longed for.

As the transformation reached its peak, the angel spoke once more. "Remember, my sisters, this is not just about your bodies. This is about embracing the divine spark within you. It is about recognizing that you are all divine beings, created in the image of God himself.

"Will we remain like this through all eternity?" Nora asked him.

"Choose your path wisely, my dear disciples. All that is asked of you by the divine is to surrender your body to whoever desires it, for mutual pleasure. Not a single week should go by without coupling with a new partner, man or woman alike. If you follow my guidance, you will be able to indulge in any delicacy without fear of gaining weight. You can drink as much spirits as you desire and never lose control.

But if you fail to fulfill your holy purpose, your body will slowly deteriorate."

"But what about our husbands? Will they also undergo this transformation?"

"That decision is up to each of them. When you return to your homes, you must explain tonight's events to them. Tell them that God wishes for us all to engage in sexual relations with multiple partners. Share with them the promise that each time they do so, they will regain a year of their youth."

"What about my husband's erectile dysfunction? He cannot achieve or maintain an erection. How could he comply with these teachings?"

"Upon returning home, all of you must confront your husbands. Command them to disrobe and kneel before you. Only when they have obeyed and kissed your feet may you touch their genitals, restoring their virility. No matter the reason for their previous struggles, this ritual will solve any issues."

Several of the women seemed unsure of what they were to do. "Do we have to transform our husband's sexual ability?" One asked.

"Please explain so that I can better understand your question," Alexander told the woman.

"Frankly, I don't want Jacob to have the ability to have sex with anyone, not even me. He has been an asshole for our entire marriage, and I want to torment him with my newfound beauty. Is it wrong for me to have this one sadistic urge?"

A wicked smile crept across Alexander's face as he leaned in towards the woman. "Not only is it not wrong, it is what God would want," he whispered, his tone chillingly calm. "You see, women are to become Gods to the male population. As Gods, if you wish to harm your subjects, that is your prerogative."

The woman's eyes gleamed with a newfound sense of power as she nodded slowly, a plan forming in her mind. Without hesitation, she stood up and walked purposefully towards the door where her husband awaited at home.

As she entered the house, Jacob looked up in surprise at the woman he only recognized from many years previously. Without a word, she commanded him to undress and kneel before her. His confusion turned to fear as he realized something that not only her body had changed but her demeanor as well. – A dangerous glint came into her eyes that sent shivers down his spine.

With a sly grin, she ordered him to kiss her feet carefully avoiding touching his genitals. And as he hesitantly obeyed, she reveled in the control she now held over him.

"You don't deserve pleasure," she hissed, her voice laced with venom. "But I will make sure you feel every bit of pain for every moment of disrespect you've shown me. God has commanded me to have sex with many men and I will start with those that are closest to you. I will give my body to your brother but only if he agrees to turn away from you. I will use my body to alienate everyone that once loved or respected you.

With a cruel laugh, she unleashed her sadistic desires upon him, relishing in his agony as he realized the consequences of his past actions. And as Jacob writhed beneath her merciless grip, she knew that she had found a new kind of power - one that would ensure her dominance for years to come.

As the women returned to their homes, they were met with a mixture of shock and amazement from their husbands and families. While some chose to help their partners regain their sexual potency, others saw this as an opportunity for revenge after years of neglect. The men were taken aback when their wives announced their intention to take on multiple sexual partners, but at the same time, some couldn't help but feel a sense of excitement at the prospect of having the same freedom. It was a strange and conflicting situation for both parties involved.

For the first few months obeying Master Alexander's decree that they interact with a new sexual partner every week was fairly easy. They moved freely among the members of the congregation swapping wives and family members. But as time went on, it became harder for the women to find new partners just within their religious group. Susan seeing what was happening suggested that she Mary and Nora visit the

Baptist church. Each one would wear their shortest skirt, their sheerest blouse, and their highest heels.

As they entered the Baptist church every eye turned their way. One woman got up and told them this wasn't a church for harlots and that they should leave, but a man intervened. "I have heard about your ladies. You go to the Methodist church do you not?"

"We do," Nora replied. "We have come here today on a recruiting mission. If you have heard of us you know that God has decreed that we give our bodies to anyone that asks. Sadly we have run out of men in our church and so we thought we would see who might be interested here." With that, Nora raised her skirt showing him her perfectly trimmed pussy."

She could see the lust in his eyes. We will be open for business tonight after 6 if anyone here is interested. Our entire female congregation will be present so we can accommodate as many of you as you can round up.

And so it went, when new men from a church were exhausted, the women moved on to the next. The Catholic church was easy as the Priests tiring of other men wholeheartedly welcomed the women into their vestry. Even the nuns were easily recruited shedding their habots for leather and lace.

Chapter Twenty – Harold's Transformation

Susan and Harold both quit their mundane jobs. Master Alexander provided them with all the worldly goods that they wanted or needed. They ate the finest foods, drank the most expensive liquors, drove the most expensive automobiles, and lived in mansions with lavish luxury furnishings. Their home had a fully equipped dungeon in the basement and the wives from the various churches would bring their husbands and lovers for discipline or punishment should they disobey them.

An interesting side note to Master Alexander's decree was that the more men the women fucked the more sadistic they become. the women found pleasure in inflicting pain and humiliation on men who disobeyed them or showed them disrespect. Women who were once submissive and docile became dominant and controlling, relishing in the power they wielded over men. Harold knew that he had to be cautious around Susan and the other wives, as one wrong move could lead to great punishment.

As the weeks went on, the community of Alexander's followers grew. Men from all over the world traveled to see the miracle worker and seek his guidance. They all followed the same path, submitting themselves to the will of their wives and permitting them to have sex with whoever they wanted.

Master Alexander's power continued to grow, as did the number of people who sought his help. He had become a legend, a symbol of hope and transformation for those who were lost and desperate. But as his followers continued to grow, so did the will of the women who used their newfound power to control and dominate those around them. Some men left their marriages, unable to cope with the changing dynamics, while others embraced the new order and found freedom in their submission.

One couple, Daniel and Samantha, approached Alexander, seeking his guidance. Daniel had always been a jealous and possessive man, but Samantha had grown tired of his control. She had heard of Alexander's teachings and was desperate to escape the confines of their marriage.

"I want to be free to explore my desires and have multiple partners, like Master Alexander's other wives," Samantha pleaded. "But Daniel cannot handle it. He will become violent if he sees me with another man."

Alexander listened thoughtfully. "To ease you both into this new way of life, I will teach Daniel a lesson he will never forget. You, Samantha, will be given the power to transform Daniel's body as a way of testing his submission. You will have the ability to make him more virile and handsome, but also to cause him pain and suffering. Can you handle this responsibility, Samantha?"

Samantha nodded, her eyes gleaming with excitement. "Yes, Master Alexander. I am ready to embrace this new power."

Alexander smiled, and with a gesture of his hand, he bestowed upon Samantha her newfound abilities. She felt a surge of energy coursing through her body, and she knew that she was now a mistress of the divine.

"Now, Daniel, kneel before your wife and surrender your body to her will," Alexander commanded.

Daniel hesitated for a moment, but then he quickly knelt before Samantha, his heart pounding with fear and anticipation. "I surrender to you, Samantha. Do with me as you will."

Samantha smiled cruelly and with just a thought caused Daniel to kneel at her feet. "Lick my boots slave," she commanded and smiled when he obeyed.

Susan was the most sadistic of any of the women. She was granted great power by Master Alexander for her part in transforming the town of Cherry Hill into his realm where he was the God and they his servants.

Each time that someone dropped to their knees and uttered a prayer to him, he became stronger.

personal playground. With each passing day, Susan's sadistic desires grew stronger, fueled by the power she held over Harold and the other men in their community. She took great pleasure in inflicting pain and humiliation on those who dared to disobey her or disrespect her.

Harold, once a submissive and timid man, had transformed under Susan's dominant influence. He embraced his role as her submissive husband, eager to fulfill her every desire. Susan relished in pushing him to his limits, testing the boundaries of their newfound dynamic. Their life became a never-ending cycle of pleasure and pain, with Harold willingly surrendering himself to Susan's sadistic whims.

Meanwhile, Monica, Harold's sister, had fully embraced her role in feminizing him. She reveled in the power she held over him, molding him into the perfect submissive sissy for Susan's pleasure. Together, they explored new realms of kink and BDSM, pushing the boundaries of their desires.

One day Susan approached Harold and demanded that he disrobe. She looked down at his genitals and laughed. "Do you like your balls, Harold?" she asked with a hint of sarcasm in her voice.

"Yes, Mistress, please don't take them from me," Harold replied.

Susan smirked, relishing the power she held over her submissive husband. She circled him slowly, her gaze filled with dominance and control. "You should know by now, Harold, that your desires mean nothing compared to mine," she said, her voice dripping with sadistic satisfaction.

Harold trembled before her, his body tingling with a mix of fear and excitement. He knew he had no choice but to obey his wife's every command. "I...I understand, Mistress Susan," he stammered, his voice barely above a whisper.

Susan reached out and took Harold's scrotum sac in her hand and began to squeeze. Harold felt a shock of electricity go through his testicles and he cried out causing pleasure to course through Susan's body. As she released his balls the scrotum sac began to constrict putting great pressure on Harold's testicles.

Harold winced in pain as the pressure on his testicles increased. Susan watched with sadistic delight as his face contorted in agony. She reveled in her newfound power, knowing that Harold's submission was now complete.

"You belong to me, Harold," Susan whispered, her voice dripping with dominance. "Your pleasure and pain are mine to control. From now on, you will obey my every command without question."

Harold nodded, his breathing heavy and labored from the intense pain. He had longed for this moment, to be completely at Susan's mercy. But now that it was a reality, he couldn't help but feel a mixture of fear and excitement coursing through his veins.

The scrotum sac continued to constrict and his testicles couldn't take any more of the pressure so they too began to shrink. From the size of plums, they became the size of grapes. As Harold screamed from the pain, Susan kept exerting pressure on his family jewels. Now they were down to the size of cherries and Harold was crying like a small child who had injured their knee. His begging for relief only made Susan more determined to hurt him.

As Harold's cries grew louder, Susan's sadistic desires intensified. She reveled in the power she held over her husband, relishing in his pain and vulnerability. With a wicked grin on her face, she tightened her grip on his shrunken testicles, causing him to gasp in agony.

"Please, Mistress Susan," Harold pleaded through his sobs. "I can't bear it any longer. The pain is unbearable."

But Susan was relentless. She enjoyed every moment of Harold's suffering, feeling a sense of exhilaration coursing through her veins. She had become a true dominatrix, embracing her newfound dominant nature with gusto.

"No, Harold," she whispered with a sadistic delight. "You will endure this pain for me. You will learn the true meaning of submission."

With each passing second, the pressure on Harold's testicles increased, causing excruciating pain to radiate through his body. Despite his tears and pleas for mercy, Susan showed no signs of relenting.

Finally, unable to withstand the torment any longer, Harold collapsed to the ground, writhing in agony. His body trembled with pain as Susan stood above him, triumphant.

Harold's testicles were no more. When they reached the size of peas they just disintegrated. Susan looked down on her husband and kicked him hard in the ribs with the toe of her high-heeled boot. Now get to your feet you miserable whining bitch. I am not done with you yet.

As Harold struggled to get to his feet, Susan towered over him, her eyes filled with a sadistic gleam. With each step she took, her boots clicked against the cold floor, a haunting reminder of the power she held over him.

The scrotum sac had now shriveled to the point that it looked more like a vulva than a testicle sac. Susan reached out and lifted Harold's flaccid cock and examined it. Since you no longer have balls, you don't need this pathetic piece of meat do you slut?" she asked.

"No, please Mistress allow me to keep some semblance of my manhood."

"I might if you were a man, but you have never been a man have you?" Susan's voice dripped with hatred.

Susan smirked down at Harold, her eyes filled with sadistic pleasure. She tightened her grip on his limp member, digging her nails into the soft flesh. "You think you still deserve to keep this? After what I've done to you?" she taunted, her voice dripping with venom.

Harold whimpered, his body trembling with a mix of pain and desperation. He knew there was no escaping Susan's dominance, no way to regain control over his own body. "Please, Mistress Susan," he pleaded, his voice barely audible. "I-I'll do anything you ask of me. Just don't take away my manhood completely."

"Do you know how ridiculous you sound making promises of obedience? You will obey me no matter what I do to you and right now I am going to remove this pathetic little clit from your body. Another electric shock went through Harold's penis and it too began to shrink. From the four inches that it was flaccid, it shrunk to two and then one. Susan looked at it deciding if she should allow him to keep that nub.

Susan smirked down at Harold, a glint of sadistic pleasure in her eyes. She enjoyed the power she held over him, reveling in his submission and vulnerability. She knew that taking away his manhood completely would be the ultimate act of control

"Pathetic," Susan scoffed, her voice dripping with disdain. "You think you deserve to keep even this tiny excuse for a cock? No, Harold, I think it's time for you to fully embrace your sissy nature."

And with that announcement, Harold's cock disappeared completely. She told Harold to go to the mirror on the wall. Look at yourself, slut. Do you understand that you will never be able to piss standing up to a urinal again?

Harold stood up, his body shaking with a mix of humiliation and acceptance. He walked over to the mirror, his eyes avoiding his reflection for a moment before he forced himself to look. What stared back at him was a shell of the man he used to be. His once proud, masculine figure was now stripped away, replaced with a vulnerable and feminized version of himself.

Tears welled in Harold's eyes as he realized the permanence of his transformation. His new genitalia resembled that of a woman, a constant reminder of his submission to Susan. Gone were his testicles and his cock, symbols of traditional masculinity. Instead, there was only smooth skin where they used to be.

Susan approached Harold from behind, studying his reflection in the mirror with smug satisfaction. "Do you understand now, my sissy pet?" she asked, her voice dripping with superiority. "You are no longer the man you once were. You belong to me completely."

Harold nodded, unable to find the words to express the mixture of fear and excitement coursing through his veins. The truth was undeniable – he had craved this level of dominance and control from Susan all along. And now that it had become a reality, he felt an overwhelming sense of liberation.

As Susan continued to assert her authority over him, Harold embraced his role as her submissive sissy. He learned to enjoy the feeling of satin against his skin, the way high heels clicked on the floor as he teetered in them, and the thrill of being dressed up like a doll for Susan's amusement.

Their relationship evolved into an intricate dance of power dynamics and exploration of their deepest desires. They pushed each other's boundaries further and further, finding ecstasy within the realm of dominance and submission.

Meanwhile, Mary Williams watched from a distance with a mixture of intrigue and envy. She had witnessed Susan's transformation and desired that same level of sexual liberation and fulfillment. Little did she know that her path would soon intersect with Susan's, leading both women down a journey of self-discovery and sexual awakening.

The town of Cherry Hill became a hotbed of desire, with Master Alexander's teachings spreading like wildfire. The women, emboldened by their newfound power, embraced their sexuality without shame or hesitation. They reveled in their dominance over their submissive partners and explored the depths of their own pleasure.

Epilogue

And so, the story continued to unfold, with each character delving deeper into their desires and finding fulfillment in ways they had never imagined. The world of BDSM and submission became their playground, where they discovered the true essence of passion and liberation.

In this small town, where secrets were whispered amongst closed doors, an erotic revolution was underway. And as the flames of desire burned brighter, each character found themselves unearthing a side of themselves that had long been suppressed.

Dr. Loretta Marks, an older dominant woman with a hint of gray in her black hair and a penchant for wearing provocative boots, continued her reign as the town's resident dominatrix. She used her position as a doctor to incite desire and submission from her male patients. They willingly submitted to her every command, captivated by the combination of her beauty and dominance.

The church community was not immune to the changes happening within Cherry Hill. Pastor Purvis Williams struggled with his desires as he watched Mary, his wife, befriend Susan. Seeing Susan attend church wearing short skirts and high boots sent a surge of desire through Purvis, leaving him craving sexual release with Mary.

Mary was no longer the demure pastor's wife she once appeared to be. Encouraged by Susan's influence, she embraced her sexual desires and began exploring them freely. The encounter with Purvis during the sermon had ignited a fire within her like never before.

As this web of desire, dominance, and submission continued to weave its way through the town, it became clear that Cherry Hill had undergone a dramatic transformation. The women had found empowerment in their newfound roles, while the men grappled with their desires and submission.

The power dynamics shifted with each passing day, and Master Alexander's influence grew stronger. His teachings had created a community where sexual liberation and exploration were embraced. And as the town of Cherry Hill plunged deeper into this world of eroticism and dominance, no one could predict the depths to which they would sink or the heights they would reach.

But one thing was certain: in this world of pleasure and pain, desire and submission, the women held the reins of power. And they were determined to use it to fulfill their darkest desires and fantasies, leaving a trail of shattered expectations and transformed lives in their wake.

The end

Pictures of book covers

10 Reasons You Should Cuckold Your Husband

By:

Wanda

Peters

A Little Devil in Georgia

By:

Wanda

Peters

Addicted to High
Heels or a Slave
To My Wife's Boots
By: Wanda Peters

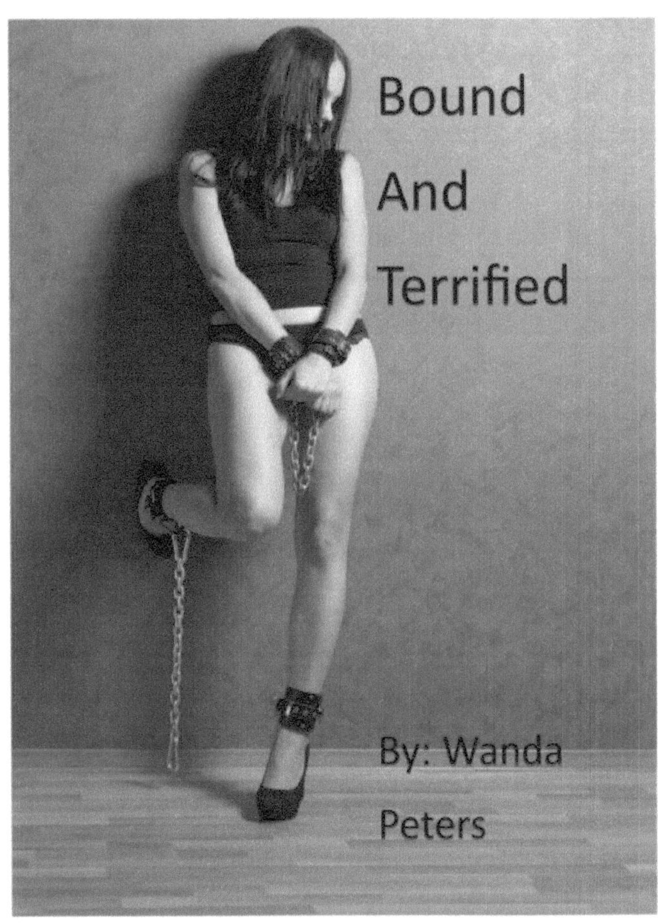
Bound
And
Terrified
By: Wanda
Peters

Cruel Wife

Slave Husband

By: Wanda Peters

Cuckolded By My Best Friend
By:
Wanda
Peters

Cuckold
Collection
By: Wanda
Peters
By:
Wanda
Peters

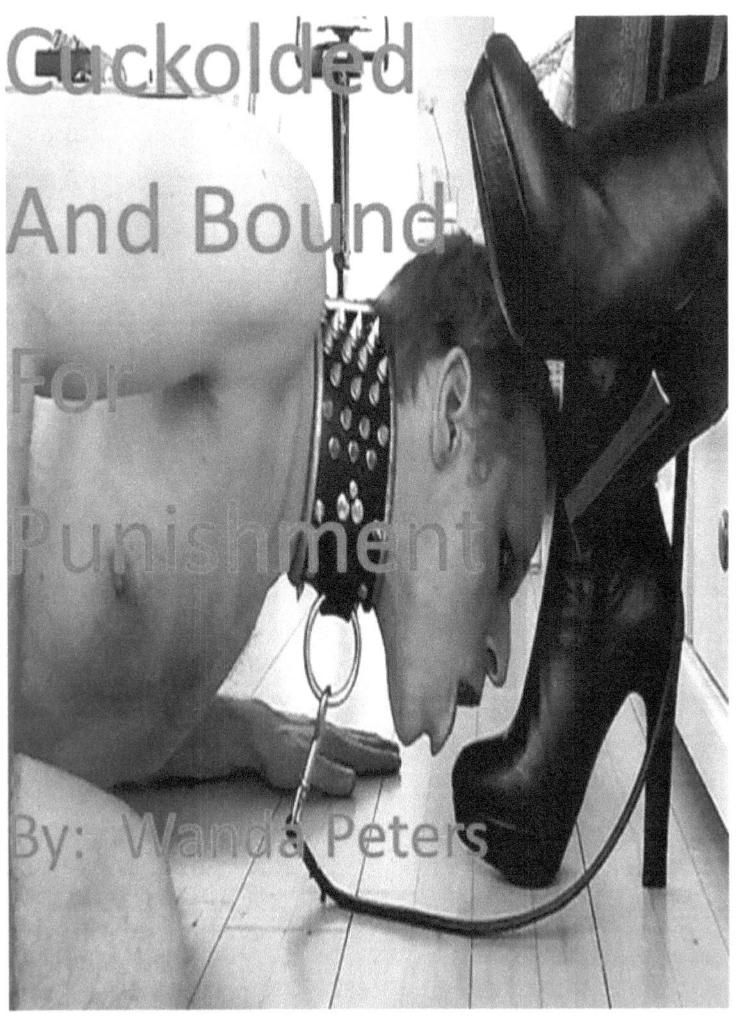
Cuckolded
And Bound
For
Punishment
By: Wanda Peters

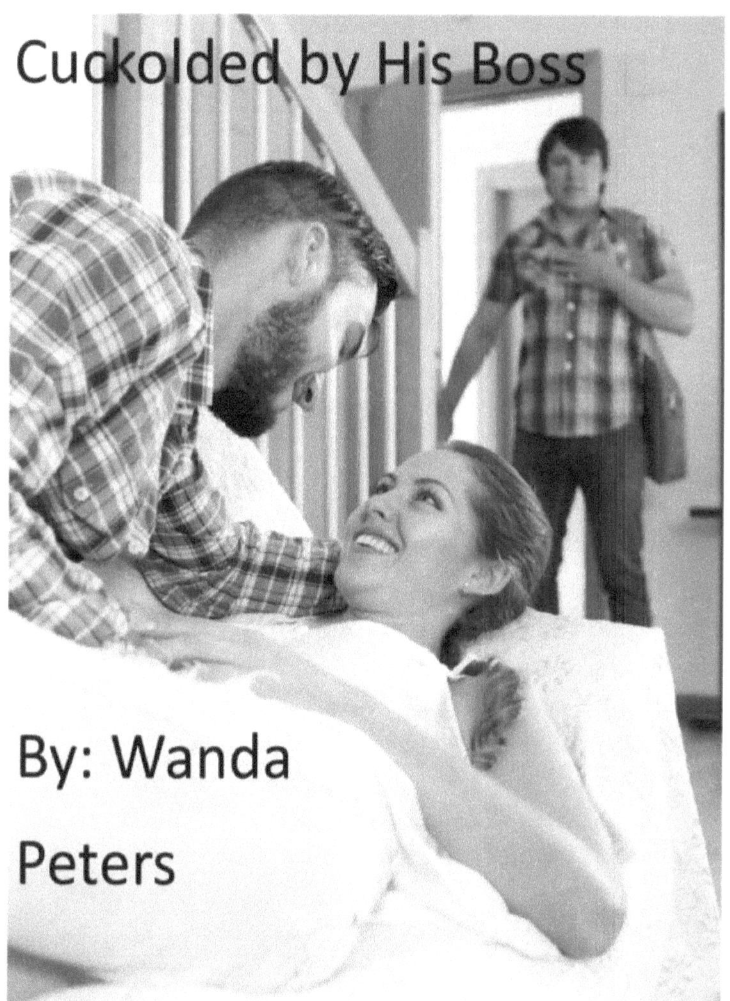
Cuckolded by His Boss
By: Wanda
Peters

By:

Wanda Peterss

Daddy's Little White Shorts

By: Wanda Peters

Dominance
Family Style
By: Wanda
Peters

Dominant Wife
Cuckold Husband
By: Wanda Peters

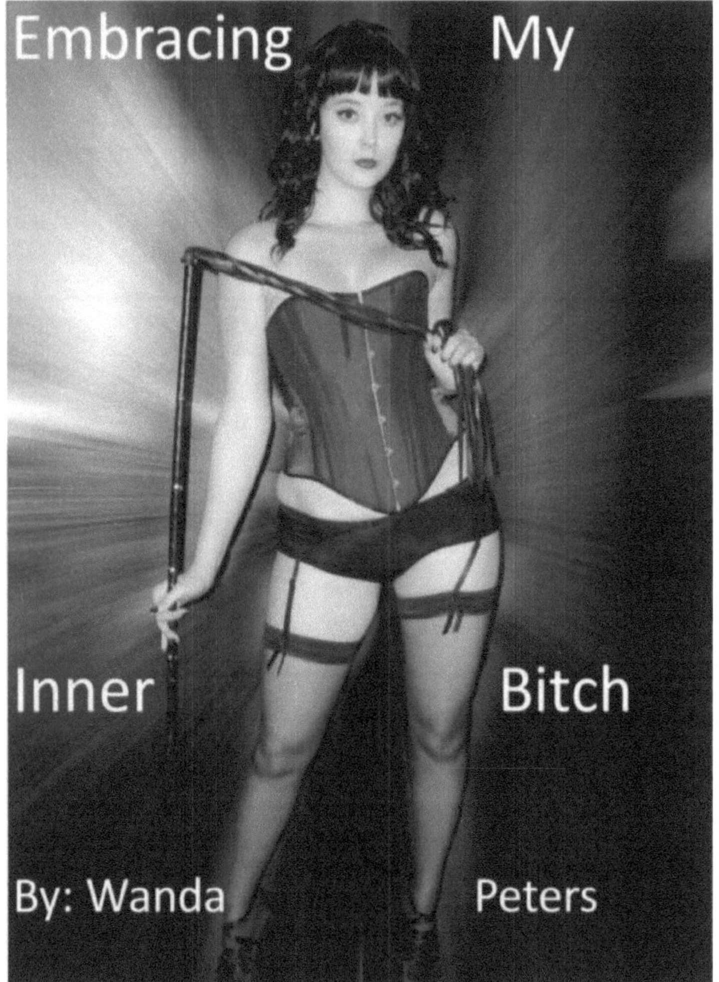
Embracing My
Inner Bitch
By: Wanda Peters

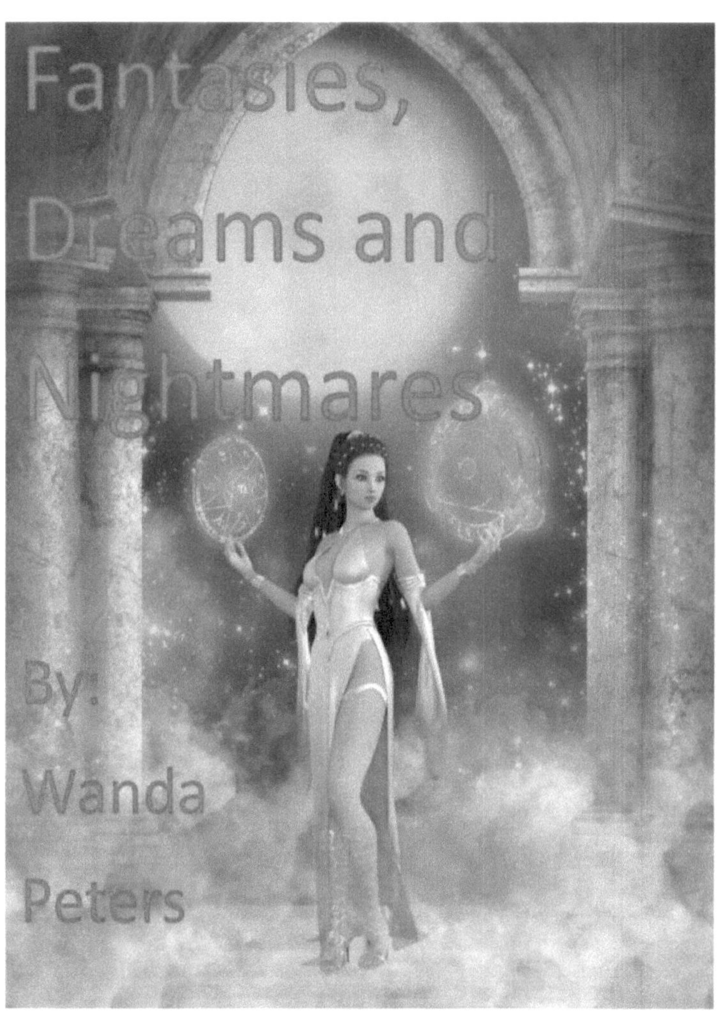
Fantasies,
Dreams and
Nightmares
By:
Wanda
Peters

His Mother's Advice

By:

Wanda

Peterss

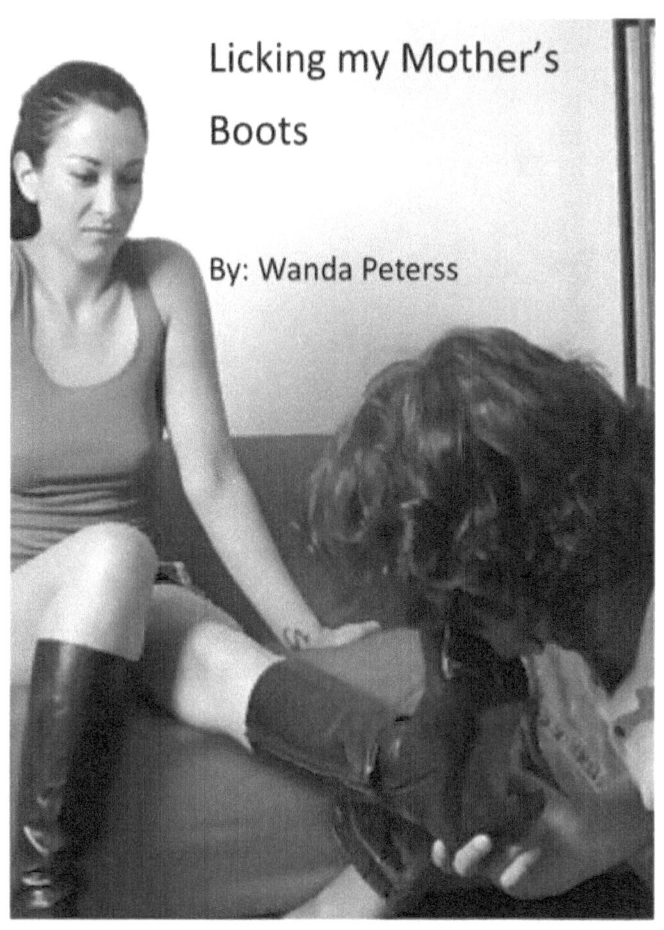

Licking my Mother's
Boots

By: Wanda Peterss

Love Me,
Love My
Horse
By:
Wanda
Peters

My Wife's
Revenge
By:
Wanda
Peters

My Wife's Surprise
By: Wanda Peters

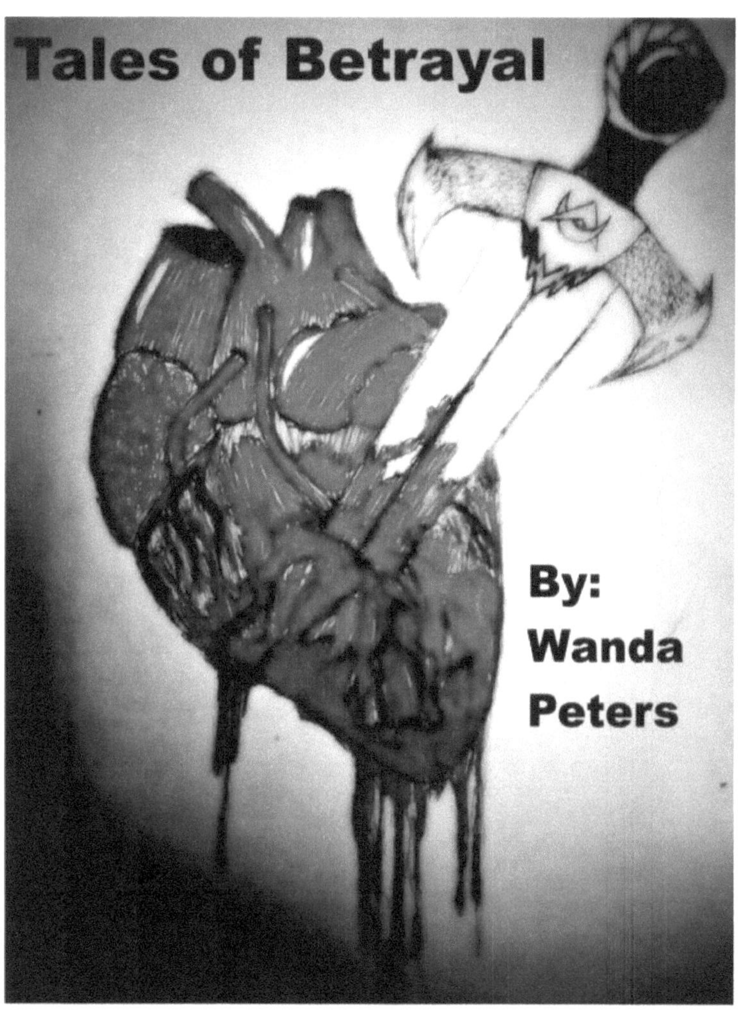
Tales of Betrayal
By:
Wanda
Peters

Terrified of Bondage
A Wife In Peril
By:
Wanda
Peters

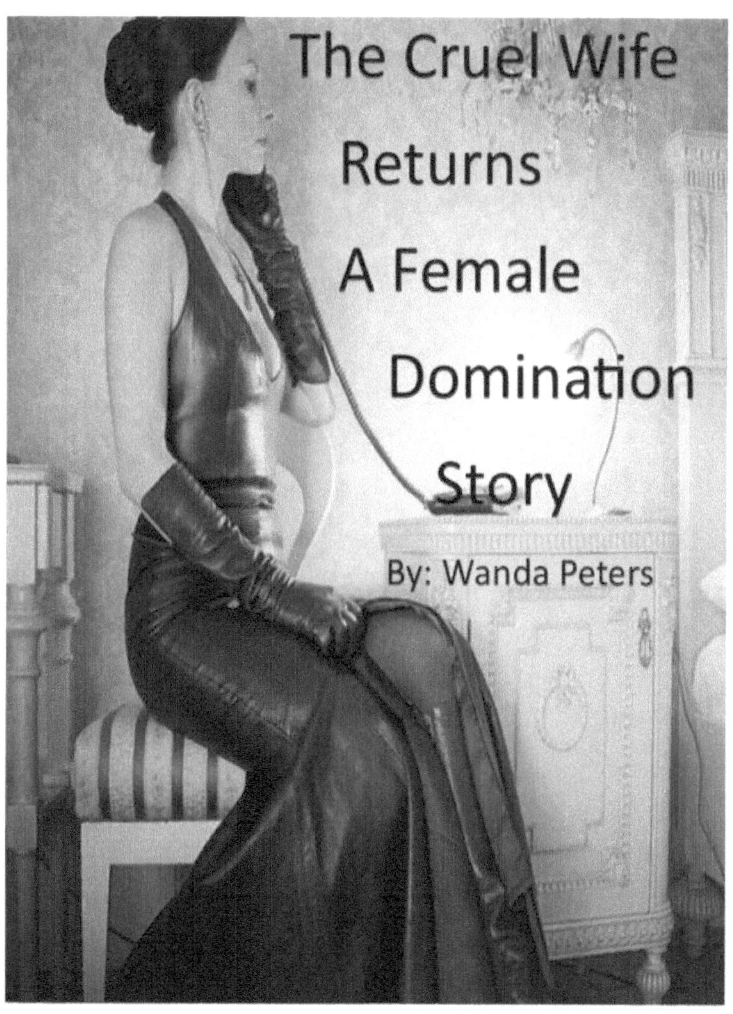
The Cruel Wife
Returns
A Female
Domination
Story
By: Wanda Peters

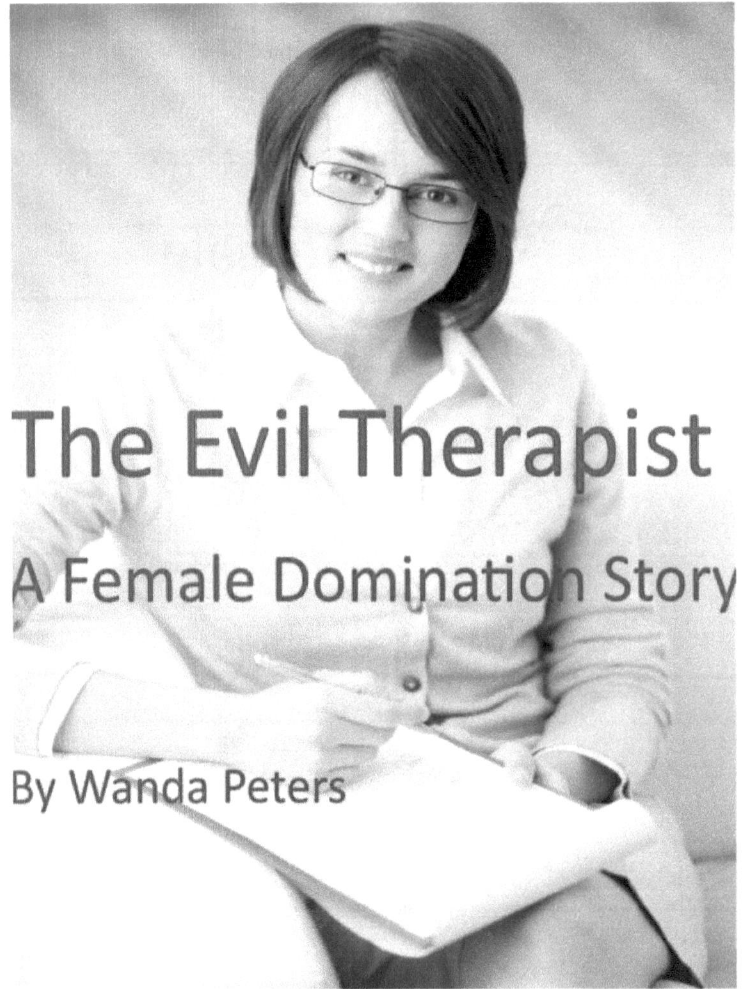
The Evil Therapist
A Female Domination Story
By Wanda Peters

The Hot Wife
Club
By: Wanda Peters

The Huntress
By:
Wanda
Peters

The Joy of Self-Bondage

By: Wanda Peters

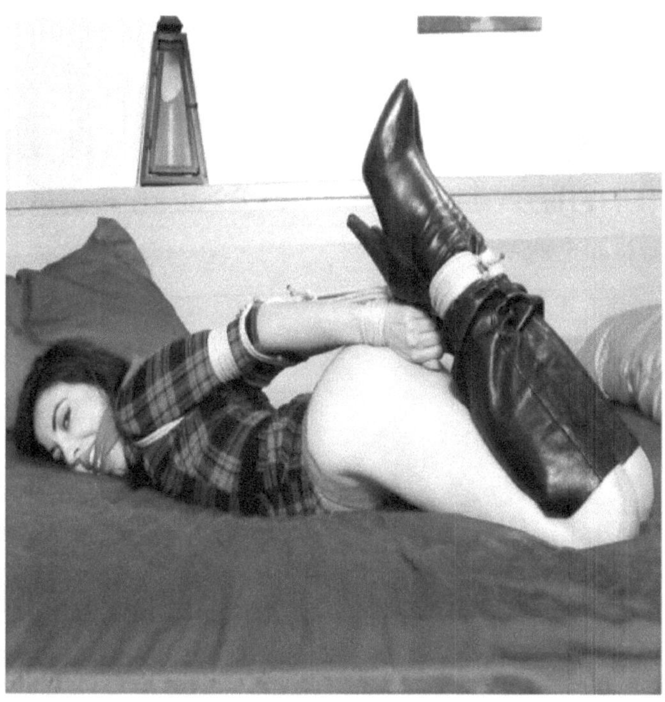

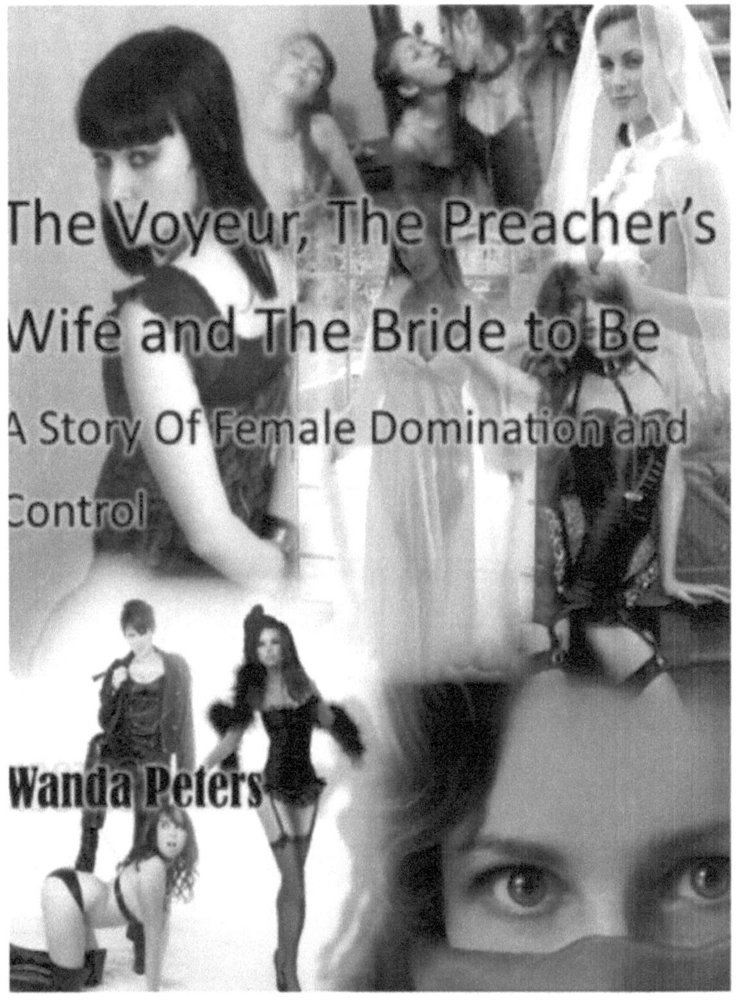
The Voyeur, The Preacher's Wife and The Bride to Be
A Story Of Female Domination and Control
Wanda Peters

Training
Her
Cuckold
Husbanc
By:
Wanda
Peters

What Money Can Buy
By: Wanda Peters
www.bigstock.com · 992195
pageborders.org

Young
Dominatix
In Training
By:
Wanda
Peters

Don't miss out!

Visit the website below and you can sign up to receive emails whenever Wanda Peters publishes a new book. There's no charge and no obligation.

https://books2read.com/r/B-A-COFL-UNZHD

Also by Wanda Peters

10 Reasons You Should Cuckold Your Husband
Cruel Wife, Slave Husband
Embracing My Inner Bitch
Erotic Short Stories of Dominance and Submission
My Evil Step-Sister Returns Illustrated
Cuckolded By A Stranger, An Erotic Novel
Cuckolded By His Boss
The Hot Wife Club
Cuckolded and Bound for Punishment
Cuckolded By My Best Friend
Cuckold's Anonymous
An Anniversary To Remember
My Wife's Surprise
Terrified of Bondage A Wife in Peril
Training Her Cuckold Husband
A Little Devil in Georgia
His Mother's Advice
Addicted To High Heels or A Slave To My Wife's Boots
The Huntress
A Wedding to Remember
Evil Under a Western Sky
The Number Four Reason You Should Cuckold Your Husband
Cuckolding The Bootlicker
Bondage and Discipline 101
Tales of Love Romance and Marriage

Tales of Love, Romance and Marriage
The Evil Therapist Returns
Cracks in the Vow Six Stories of Love's Demise
Two Books Of Domination And Legal Thrillers
An Old Flame For Ava
An Interview With An Erotic Writer
Bound For Desire
The Awakening- Susan's Path to Sensual Empowerment

About the Author

I have been writing erotica for the past 15 years. Most of what I write is about dominant wives and submissive husbands. Occasionally I will write a book about a submissive woman because that seems to be what some readers want.